The Mustanger and the Lady

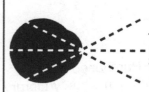

This Large Print Book carries the
Seal of Approval of N.A.V.H.

THE BRANDIRON SERIES

THE MUSTANGER
AND THE LADY

DUSTY RICHARDS

WHEELER PUBLISHING
A part of Gale, a Cengage Company

Farmington Hills, Mich • San Francisco • New York • Waterville, Maine
Meriden, Conn • Mason, Ohio • Chicago

LIBRARY OF CONGRESS CATALOGING-IN-PUBLICATION DATA

Names: Richards, Dusty, author.
Title: The mustanger and the lady / by Dusty Richards.
Description: Large print edition. | Waterville, Maine : Wheeler Publishing, 2017. |
    Series: The Brandiron series | Series: Wheeler Publishing large print western
Identifiers: LCCN 2017021823| ISBN 9781432841935 (hardcover) | ISBN 1432841939
    (hardcover)
Subjects: LCSH: Large type books. | GSAFD: Western stories.
Classification: LCC PS3568.I31523 M87 2017 | DDC 813/.54—dc23
LC record available at https://lccn.loc.gov/2017021823

Published in 2017 by arrangement with Galway Press, an imprint of Oghma Creative Media

Printed in Mexico
1 2 3 4 5 6 7 21 20 19 18 17

For Pat

FOREWORD

I never dreamed I would get to book number 150, but here I am, and it's a special milestone for me. This story was originally written a few years back. I couldn't find a publisher for it back then, but last summer I took it off a dusty shelf and reexamined it. I saw a few things that needed touching up, and it sure needed some editing — but the book moved and excited me just as it had years ago. My publishers, Casey Cowan and Gil Miller of Oghma Creative Media, read the fresh edition and said, "Wow, this is a real John Wayne western."

That was the finest flattery I had heard about one of my books. I always was a big fan of the Duke. This is the desert scene I grew up in and shows the transformation of the Arizona geography from desert to the tall pines. I've ridden on horseback over most of this landscape. I saw all that when I first reread the copy and revised it. I hope you enjoyed it as much as I have.

Now what's put the frosting on the cake? A movie studio has taken an option out to turn it into a film. We all may get to see it played out on the silver screen. I'll sure be there eating popcorn when it gets there, too. I spent many Saturday afternoons in my youth watching Gene, Hobby and Roy gallop across the screen. Be nice to have my name in the credits rolling up the list.

When I originally wrote this book I recalled long ago going to the Skeleton Cave Site in Arizona. This is a place where a small band of Apache renegades were slain by the US Army. Apache men, women and children took shelter in a cavern. The soldiers trailing them followed, and soon located their hideout. The report said they were asked to surrender, but declined. The attackers then fired a barrage of bullets into the cave's roof, which ricocheted down upon the holdouts like rain until all were dead. A few partial skulls still littered the cavern floor with other human bones when I visited. It made me sick, thinking about the death of innocent women and children in this crypt. But I also kept in mind that lots of innocents fell in the path of these people's wrath, too.

This is a very secluded place in that vast

dry desert country. My party hiked in with our own water and food in our backpacks. I couldn't find the way back today unless it was mapped, and my arthritis complains too much to try. South of there is the Superstition Country where the Lost Dutchman's Mine waits for someone to unlock the door. I didn't find it, either, but this is the country — the life — that made me want to write westerns. The West wasn't just black and white, cowboys and indians, good guys and bad *hombres.* It was just people, doing their best day by day like the rest of us. No hero is without a dark side, and every villian has a mother, and the rough country of the West had a habit of making things like right and wrong murky as a muddy stream. Just ask those Apaches in the cave, or the soldiers that killed them.

Thanks for being my supporters. If you have any questions email me at dusty richards@cox.net. I love to hear from my fans, and I'll answer any letter you send. You can also check out my website at dustyrichardslegacy.com, and find me on Facebook.

— *Dusty Richards*
December 29, 2015
Springdale, Arkansas

ONE

Distorted heat waves rose from the desert floor. A mirage of silver water shimmered under the midday sun while hot gusts of wind and dust devils danced across the basin. The intensity of the forge-like blasts forced Vince Wagner to squint at the distant saw-edged mountains to the west.

In the web of his left hand, he caught his high-crowned hat by the curled brim and removed it. He wiped the perspiration from his forehead on his shirtsleeve. His attention remained centered on the actions of the half-broke roman-nosed dun under him. Despite their long, hot ride through the cholla and rocks, the green-broke gelding still tensed every once in a while, as if ready to buck. The horse's unpredictability rode foremost in his mind. He reset the weathered gray hat back to shade his eyes.

Halted on a rise, a moving object on the little-used road to the Murphy Mine caught his attention. He stood up in the stirrups and stretched his over six-foot frame while he tried to determine the identity of the stranger.

Whoever the subject was, they were wearing something bright green. The color puzzled him. Though he squinted hard against the glare, he couldn't totally identify the distant object. One part looked like a limping horse, but his inability to figure out more than that bothered him. He tried to neck rein the half-broke horse around, and finally, filled with impatience, he plowreined him, anxious to find out more about the intruder.

"Easy, stupid!" he cautioned the gelding. "We'll ride down there and see who that is."

Talking to his horse was a habit he'd acquired since moving to the Hondo Mountains to chase mustangs and run a few cows under his own brand. There were times the sound of his own voice was his only company. But the part he liked best was none of the horses ever talked back.

The mustang swelled beneath him. He tensed, ready for the horse's next trick. Instead the dun settled into a long-strided lope. When he drew closer, the person in the bright green clothing stopped and looked back at him across the greasewood and tall cactus. Then as if seized with panic, the individual in question mounted the crippled horse and began whipping it from side to side with the reins to get it to go.

What was wrong with them? Confused, he frowned as he drew closer.

The rider proved to be a girl in a green silk dress. He could see her shapely, bare legs as she sat astride her unwilling mount. He loped his dun up behind her. She twisted around to view him and stark terror was written on her face. She turned back, her long dark brown hair in rolled curls that bounced on her bare shoulders.

Lashing with her reins, she punished the lame horse into a crippled trot.

"Hold up!" he shouted, standing in the stirrups as he drew alongside her.

"No way, mister!" An expression of determination on her face, she resumed booting the spent mount.

"Whoa." He scowled at her reaction to his orders.

He grabbed her bridle and stopped her.

"Let go of my horse or I'll —" Her face contorted into a mask of anger. "Where do you get the gall to stop me? Let go of my horse this minute!"

"Ease off. I'm not going to hurt you." He

13

frowned at the streaked rouge-and-trail-dust-smudged image. Half of her milk-white breasts were exposed, and it was a marvel the low-cut dress was even up that high. But the sun-scorched raw skin on her shoulders and arms drew a sympathetic cringe from him.

His gaze met the palest blue eyes he could ever recall. But there was no denying her origin from her appearance and her clothing. She was some sort of a dance hall girl. A pang of disappointment soured his discovery.

"Let go of that!" she demanded. "Get away from me."

"Why? It's six miles up these ruts to Murphy's Mine. Besides he ain't there. There ain't a bit of water up there either, and you look to me like you need some shade." Dance hall gal or not, he couldn't let her die out there or go on punishing the poor horse.

"Why don't you mind your own damn business!" She began slapping at his arm where he held her bridle reins. Her even white teeth bared, her mouth was set in a determined slant.

"I'm trying to help." He leaned back from her wild blows. How could one person try his patience so much?

14

"Let go! I don't need your damn help!" She flailed him on his shoulder and arm harder with her reins.

"Well, that horse damn sure needs my help," he said, his impatience growing by the second at her irrational behavior.

"He isn't yours, he's mine. Get away from me!"

"Listen —" Filled with rage at her belligerence, he pushed the dun into her horse's side and grabbed her by the waist. His efforts pulled her screaming and kicking out of the saddle.

This squalling, kicking female reminded him of a captured wild mustang.

He quickly discovered that he needed to be on the ground to ever gain control of her. To dismount would be taking a chance his half-broke horse might run off and leave him afoot. But there was no way to suppress the cursing, struggling hellcat he'd captured without stepping down. With the hard ribs of her corset in his encircling arm, he dismounted as she screeched vehemently and thrashed in his hold.

Her fist connected with his left eye. In a galaxy of stars from the blow, he never lost his grip on her or the reins. The time had come for him to put an end to the nonsense she was dealing him. In disgust, he dropped the reins and spun her over his knee. Too late, she tried to stop what he planned and squalled for help. With his flat hand, he applied hard, palm-stinging whacks to her bottom.

"Don't hurt me. Please don't," she cried, trying to reach back to protect herself. "I'll be good. Anything — I promise. Oh! That hurts." She tried to twist away to avoid any further punishment.

"Then settle down." He stood her up on her feet.

The front of her dress had sunk dangerously low. She wiggled it up, and gave him a hard look. "So who are you?"

"Most folks call me Vince." He tested his tender eye with a fingertip.

With narrow slits for eyes to critically appraise him up and down she asked. "Do you work for Allison?"

"Allison who?" He shook his head in wonderment at her. He didn't know any Allison in that country.

"Never mind," she said in a sharp tone. "What are you planning to do with me?"

"First take that horse away from you. He needs some care. Poor thing has been rode to death. His right hind hoof either has rock in his frog or he's bruised it. That ain't no way to treat a horse." He frowned at her ignorance of animals.

"What about me?" she asked. Seated on the ground, she pulled on her high heeled, button-up shoes that she'd lost in their ruckus. For them to fall off, Vince decided, she must have had them unbuttoned.

"To be right honest, I'm worried more about the horse," he said, attempting to retain his anger toward her. Carefully, he captured the reins to his own dun, grateful he hadn't run off. Maybe some of his ground tie training had stuck with the animal.

"Are you crazy? You can't just leave me here!" Her hands perched on her hips in defiance. "That's horse stealing. You can't do this to me."

"I didn't ask you to come here," he said with a slow nod. "Seems to me like you got here all right by yourself. I guess you can go back too."

"Aw, come on now, Buster. It's miles back to that dried up store." She shook her head in disbelief. "You can't just leave me out here alone. Buster, you come back here."

"My name's Vince," he said, stepping into the saddle. "Lady, I'll take this horse to my place, let him heal up, and as soon as he's well you can have him back."

"When's that?" Her voice cracked.

He shrugged. "Oh, in a couple of weeks."

"Aw, come on," she pleaded, looking around. "This will be murder to leave me out here on foot."

"Well if you can find your way, my outfit is about six miles over this hill at the foot of Hondo Mountain. Come by and see about his recovery." He used his spur to nudge the dun on up the hill.

"Don't leave me here." Wobbling along on her high heels after him and protesting every step of the way. "Mister you hear me? Don't leave me here to die."

"Have a nice walk," he said over his shoulder as his dun cat-hopped up the steep grade with him leading the bay.

"Aw, this is crazy. I can't walk six miles," she argued with herself, busy looking for a new place to put her next step.

On top of the hill and far enough from the edge she could not see him he dismounted and hitched the horse to a mesquite bush. A little walking might settle her down. Amused, he listened to her lamenting words as she struggled up the grade. He lifted the pony's hoof to check it.

"You can't do this to me Buster, I'm afraid of snakes. Wait for me please. Oh hell these damn shoes."

He flipped out the rock wedged in the

18

bay's frog and let him put it down to test it. The he ran his hand down the horse's hind leg. The animal would heal in a few weeks.

Seated cross-legged on the ground, he waited until she managed to reach the flat. Hands on her knees and bent over, she gulped for air. "Oh, please don't leave me."

"My name's Vince, it ain't Buster."

Out of breath, she blinked her eyes as if this was no big thing. "I'm sorry, Vince. But where do you get off stealing my horse?"

"I'm treating him."

"Is he well? Can I have him now?"

He shook his head. "Nope. He's still sore footed from that rock. He ain't going nowhere for a while."

"Now listen —"

"No, you listen," he said. "You settle down or I'll whip your butt till you do cry. What's your name?"

"My name's Julie." She gasped for breath, her face pale from exertion of the hill climb.

"Well, Julie, what do you want to do now?"

"You're serious." Straightening, she looked taken aback.

"I am. Now if you'll behave, we'll try to ride this crazy dun double back to my place. I'm warning you, he's only about that far from bucking us off." He held his thumb and forefinger an inch apart to show her.

19

Rising to his feet, he brushed off the seat of his pants and went after the horses.

"Oh, fine," she said, hopelessly struggling in her heels and wrestling her dress up for the last twenty steps. "Now I'm going to get bucked off in these big rocks."

"Not if we're careful." Vince mounted the dun and extended his arm down for her. She hoisted up her dress, and with his arm for assistance, swung up behind him on the saddle.

Jerking on the bit, he checked the impatient dun twice to make him behave. All the time he wondered if the horse would tolerate two riders. When everything appeared to be settled, he rode in close to her horse to catch the reins.

"Is he going to buck?" she asked apprehensively.

"Not if we're lucky."

"Good." She put her arms around his middle with the familiarity that they belonged there. "Where are we going?"

"My place."

"Just so I don't have to walk in these shoes." She sounded real weary.

"Are you lost?" he asked, standing up in the stirrups to lean forward and adjust the bridle chinstrap.

"Oh, I was just out riding." She sounded evasive.

"Looks more like you're running away from something to me." He touched his sore eye. Damn, grown men had hit him with less force than she had.

"I don't figure it's any of your damn business!" she said. "Besides I'll pay you."

"For what?" He glanced down at her bare white knee behind his own. The full skirt of the bright green dress was bunched up high to accommodate her being astride.

"Haven't you ever seen a woman's leg before?" she asked sarcastically.

"A time or two." His face heated up.

"How much will l owe you when my horse is well?"

"I don't know yet. He'll be a couple of weeks mending."

"What do you do up here, anyway?" She sounded braver. Having released him, she hung onto the leathers holding his bedroll and slicker on behind the saddle.

"I mustang." Vince watched the distant mountainside. A slight movement in the chaparral was obvious to him.

"What're you looking at?" she asked.

"Didn't you see him? There's a big cat up on that mountain."

"Are there many of them around here?"

21

she asked in a subdued voice.

"Quite a few," he offered and glanced down at her bare knee before looking ahead again.

"That's just great! Mountain lions and a woman beater. I must really be in a fine place. Don't stop. I promise I'll try to be nice." She gave a loud sigh of exasperation. "Why did I ever leave Goldfield?"

He half turned struck with disbelief.

"You rode here from Goldfield?"

"No, a year ago I worked there."

"I figured you come from Pinion or Potter's Crossing."

"Sure," she mumbled evasively.

"Which one?" The dun descended the steep trail into the dry wash.

"Never mind." She locked her arms around him again to keep her balance.

"Last Chance Saloon?" he asked off the top of his head.

"Sure," she said.

"I'll take you back there at the end of the week. I've got this horse and three others I'm breaking for a rancher."

"Who's that?" she asked, squirming a little behind him.

"Tom Watson. Owns the Bar T. I break a few head for him."

"Guess I've never heard of him."

The horse slid down the last few feet into the dry wash streambed. She lost her balance and fell sideways. In desperation she grabbed him to save falling off.

"Get your feet out of his flank!" he shouted as the dun ducked his head.

His warning was too damn late. The green horse broke in two, with her holding on to him for dear life. The next moment they were seated on a sand bar in the dry streambed.

"What did I tell you?" he demanded, watching the dun high kicking and bucking away. When she didn't answer, he glanced over at her struggling with the low cut dress and wincing at the pain when the stiff material gouged her sunburned skin.

"I damn sure didn't do it on purpose," she said. "What do we do now?"

"Walk." He slapped at his bat wing chaps in disgust. "Unless we can catch him."

"That horse doesn't like you," she said, pushing herself up with determination. At the final point she shoved his shoulder. "Let me go catch him, and then we can ride on to your place."

He rose to his feet, shaking his head. "One snort of that gawdawful perfume of yours, and he'll run to the next territory."

"So you don't like my perfume, huh? We'll

23

see what I can do about capturing that horse of yours." She took off her high-heeled shoes in disgust and set out barefooted down the sandy wash.

A full hundred feet behind her, he listened to her coax the horse. "Whoa, you dumb ass. I'm damn tired of this walking. You just stand there and I'll come get you."

A confident smile on his lips, he stopped and folded his arms over his chest, watching her almost reach the trailing reins. She'd never catch him. Not many folks could do a damn thing with that stupid horse. He'd spent more time than he liked to admit fooling with him.

The dun gave a great snort. Probably smelled her perfume. Amazed, he watched her snatch the leather reins and secure them before the dun spooked back like a booger was after him. She half ran in a large circle, clutching the reins and being dragged by the green-broke horse. In a flash he rushed to her aid.

"You didn't do half bad." He scowled at the dun for all his traitorous actions, including stopping for her.

"Convincing men is my business." She laughed aloud with her head thrown back.

"I reckon so," he said, not overly impressed with her brag.

24

"I'll make you a deal. I'll just call you Cowboy, and you can call me whatever," she said, sounding very sure of herself.

"Fine, Lady," he said, a little embarrassed by her brassy ways.

"Most men call me honey or baby or darling." She acted disappointed at his selection of names. Standing on one foot then the other in the hot sand, she impatiently waited for him to remount the horse.

"Lady sounds good enough for me." He reached down to hoist her up. With an effortless lift, he placed her on the seat behind him.

"I know. I know," she said. "Keep my heels out of his flank."

She squeezed him so hard he could feel the shape of her breasts against his back. The notion of that made him anxious.

"Do you bring girls home all the time?" she asked, her tone flippant.

"No ma'am, I enjoy the quiet out here."

"Oh." She wiggled against the back of the saddle. "A woman hater."

"No ma'am. I just like my peace and quiet."

"You ever been with a woman?" she asked.

He never answered her smart mouth. At that point he put spurs to the dun and sent up him cat-hopping up the trail. Frantically,

25

she clung to him like death. This time if the dun bucked, he damn sure wasn't going off. The sooner he got the horse healed and her gone, the sooner he expected to return to the solitude he enjoyed.

TWO

Sprawled beneath a half-dozen gnarled cottonwoods, his ranch headquarters consisted of a yellowed canvas tent, another piece of cloth stretched over a rectangular post frame for further shade, and a post-brush corral. Beyond the camp itself, several live springs fed a large tank of sweet water. Vince couldn't pronounce the Apache's name for the place. He suspected the title was for the tules or cattails that grew in profusion around the water's edge.

"Looks real homey," she commented with distaste as she wiggled up the frontline of the dress.

"That's Hondo Mountain. I call this Cottonwood Springs. My homestead claim takes in the springs and all this," he said, busy undoing the girth on the dun. Why did he even bother to explain it to her? Sooner she was out of his life the better it would be for his own peace of mind. For a dance hall girl, she sure had snooty ways. But he'd met her kind before. They were all damn self-important.

"What do you do for excitement?" She looked around.

Her words could certainly grate on him. He shook his head, putting his saddle on the rack. Disinclined to even answer her, he went to unsaddle her horse since she'd made no effort.

"Do you have any whiskey?" she asked, sashaying around like she expected to find something different than what she saw at first.

"No, drank it up last winter when I had the chills. Sorry about that."

"Oh, medicine." She snickered, blocking his way as he finished unsaddling her horse.

He paused and drew a deep breath. "You don't have to like it here. You don't have to stay here. This is my outfit. Lord, I couldn't afford to much more than dance one time with someone like you, if that's what I really wanted to do. But if you stay here, you can help do chores. Here put this up." He shoved the saddle and blanket into her arms. "Put it over on those racks."

At first, her blue eyes looked shocked, then anger rose in them. "What else do you expect me to do?"

"Make yourself useful. Build a fire, heat some water for *frijoles* and coffee." He motioned toward the fire pit with pots hanging across it.

"I'm not hardly dressed to be the camp squaw." She started off with the saddle, the blanket piled on top of it.

"You can start the fire in that outfit." He considered her sunburn. Her shoulders and arms must be ablaze. "Does that sunburn hurt much?"

"I can stand it," she said in a little voice.

He didn't believe her. Why did she have to act so damn tough all the time?

"I know a kind of cactus pad that will help heal it." He tried to recall how far away the best plants for that purpose were. "I'll go get some. It will help thc burning."

"Yes, thank you," she said, taken aback by his concern.

Her words made him pause. She did have some manners. Perhaps his notion to doctor her sunburn had brought them out.

The trip for the medicinal plants was short. He crossed the wash and found the bed of cactus. When he returned, she was on her knees with a pile of twigs and some pieces of ironwood. She looked up at him for help.

"I need a match," she said.

He squatted down, setting the spiny slabs on the ground. He fished a match from his vest pocket. With a swift sweep on the seat of his jeans, he lighted the sulfurous stick and carefully cupped it until the flame began to consume the small fuel. Slowly, the small fire licked upward into her larger twigs. Satisfied the fire would burn, he turned and faced her. For a brief moment he met her gaze. The deep pools of silver ice appeared to shimmer like a mirage on the desert. For the first time he noted some compassion in her look.

"Will that cactus stuff burn me?" she asked in a soft voice.

He shook his head, still fascinated with his glint of insight about her.

"I've got a chair," he said, raising up, wanting to escape the hold staring at her was beginning to have on him.

When he returned with the canvas camp-stool, he handed it to her. She had hung two pots of water on the iron hooks over the fire. At least she might be trying to help. He busied himself peeling the skin and spines off the flat slabs of cactus.

"How does that work?" she asked, looking dubiously at the process.

"Damned if I know." With juice on the tips of two fingers he cautiously touched her bare shoulder.

She winced but did not cry out. Heat radiated from her skin as he slowly expanded his coverage.

"Hurting bad?" he asked.

"That's cooler," she said, holding her breath.

"I figure you've hurt a lot over this."

She nodded her head. "I've hurt a lot, period."

That made sense. A dance hall doxie's life was not one he'd care to have to experience. Finally, he stopped his application. The tops of her shoulders and bare back were all he cared to cover. Besides the whole business of rubbing her skin made him anxious.

"Here you can do the rest." He handed her the cactus pulp.

Her haughty laughter seemed to challenge him. "Suit yourself."

She grinned openly and began to rub it on her throat and exposed bustline.

"You better put some on your face," he said, though he doubted that the medicine could work on top of the caked makeup.

"Right, but I'll need to wash it first."

"I'll get some water. I've probably got a shirt and a pair of britches you can wear. They'd be too big but —"

"Yes, anything but this dress," she agreed. "Wait. Come back here and unhook me."

He drew a deep breath. He wasn't certain just what she expected of him. His empty stomach rolled at the prospect of what she wanted him to do.

"Come on, with my sunburn, I can't reach back there. I won't bite you. Undo my dress."

His fingers fumbled with the buttons. He tried not to look and was relieved she held the dress up in front. The lacing of the white corset was soon exposed.

"You'll have to undo the rest."

"Rest?" he asked.

"Undo the corset too. Please?"

Vince shook his head and drew a deep breath. His clumsy fingers fumbled at the cord. The line between her sunburn and the unblemished creamy-white skin was very apparent. She wasn't bigger than a minute compared to his own size. He was unsure the purpose of the corset, except he knew all dance hall girls wore them, at least the high-class ones.

"You can change in the tent." He motioned with his hand. "Those clothes are laid out in there."

"Sure, Cowboy." Hugging her dress up, she flounced off to the tent.

While she changed he went to the basin to get a canvas pail of water. Her perfume still burnt the lining in his nose. The bucket full, he paused before he stood up in the long shadows of evening . . . there was no way she could endanger his security and freedom. He shook his head as he rose. That was long ago, though, and he'd buried the memories from back then deep.

He almost laughed when he saw her emerge from the tent. His shirt came below her knees, exposing her shapely bare legs, and he chided himself for being so attracted by them. They seemed to always draw his attention. She walked very gingerly in her bare feet.

"I'll need a belt or a rope to keep your pants up," she said with a laugh.

"I'll find you one," he said.

"And some shoes?" she asked quietly.

"Guess we could make you some squaw boots."

"Oh, yes, just what I need. I can be Little Squaw," she said sarcastically. "What now?"

"You can either make supper or water the horses," he said.

"How do you water them?" she asked.

"Lead them down to the tank. Let them drink."

"I'll put on my shoes," she said wryly.

Vince busied himself adding brown beans to the boiling water and grinding coffee. He glanced once after her but she seemed quite capable of taking two horses down the hill and back. The high heels must be hurting her ankles the way she twisted them about every step.

His food and coffee on the fire, he undid the heavy bull-hide chaps and hung them over his saddle. Then he squatted by the fire where he could eye the cooking and rolled himself a cigarette. Using a smoldering twig from the fire, he ignited the cylinder and drew on it slowly. Enjoying the settling luxury of nicotine, he blinked as he saw her returning leading both horses. Her clean face gleamed in the red rays of sundown. She'd washed all the makeup away.

"Say, I'm ready for those squaw boots," she said with a wide grin.

Vince just nodded. Without all that cake, she was prettier than he'd imagined she would be.

They ate supper in silence. He glanced a time or two at her small bare feet. There was enough leather in his trunk to make her some foot gear. But what was she doing lost in his country?

"You better put some of that juice on your face too," he reminded her.

She looked up at him as if to question his words. "I guess it would help. My shoulders feel much better."

"I knew it would work. You want to tell me what you're doing out here?" Vince finally asked.

"I'm prospecting for gold." She didn't look up from her plate.

"Nope. You aren't dressed for it. And you're too far away from a dance hall to just be taking a ride."

"I'm not wanted by the law."

"Good." He rose up to take the coffee pot off the hook to refill their tin cups. He used his kerchief for a hot holder.

"Actually I heard of a gold strike —"

"I'm talking straight to you lady. You ain't doing that with me." He towered over her.

She quickly agreed with a nod. "You don't need my troubles, Cowboy. You've got your own outfit. Who knows? Someday you may have thousands of cattle."

Yes, he intended to do just that. Was she lying about the law not being after her? Had she done something criminal?

She gave a great sigh and exhaled. "All right, I'm a bald-face liar. The last place I worked was Kyle Allison's Wild Horse Saloon at New Field."

He noticed a slight tremble as she sat on

35

the ground staring into the fire.

"That's a hard two days' ride from here," Vince said, intensely speculating on her origin.

"Three," she corrected him. "Some months back, Kyle Allison took a liking to me. He poured double eagles in my palm. See we all look — I mean girls in my profession look for the big spenders to take us in. Then we don't have to hustle every grubby miner in camp. In fact, he kinda set me up in his office. You could call that easy street." She paused and slowly shook her head. "You still want to hear it?"

"Sure."

"Listen, you round up horses and break them and sell them. I round up men, entertain them, and collect money for it. It's just a job."

"Go on," he said, feeling uncomfortable under her hard gaze, despite the dwindling evening light.

"I was in bed. They must have thought I was sleeping. Allison and his henchmen were talking about killing this miner and jumping his claim. I was scared, Cowboy. Listen, they'd kill a whore for a damn sight less than knowing she might be a witness against them."

"Did they kill him?" He wanted her to

continue.

"Yes. This old miner Gustafson turned up dead in two days. They said he fell off a cliff and smashed in his head. I knew his head was caved in before he was thrown down. That's how they planned it. Then two of his gunmen accused me of listening to their conversation. I was petrified."

She gave a toss of long curls to get them back off her shoulders. "I overheard them tell Allison they should get rid of me. That I knew too much. He told them he'd find out what I knew. But Allison had to go to Wickenburg on pressing business that morning, so I bought a horse and left. I mean I was scared."

"What did you eat?"

"A pair of cowboys fed me the first day at a line shack. Yesterday, a prospector gave me some food. He told me if I kept going west I'd get on the stage road."

"You missed it. You figure those guys will get on your trail?"

"Yes. They know I know about the murder now. But I'm headed for Colorado or Montana. They won't go that far."

He shook his head. "You left a trail a mile wide wearing that dress. Do you want more coffee? Must be two more cups left."

"Think I left an obvious trail?" She held

out her cup for him to pour.

"Yes, I do. Do you have a gun for your own defense?" He got to his feet to reach the coffee pot.

"No. I couldn't use one if I had it." She looked crestfallen, but he'd surmised part of her toughness was a bluff anyway.

"You better learn how." He hung the pot back.

"You think I should?"

"Lady," he said, dropping back on the stool, "if you're the link between them and the murder, I figure they're already on your trail."

Julie drew a deep breath and sighed. "I better leave at sunup. Sell me a horse."

"How far will you get? If you'd gone up that canyon to the Murphy Mine where there's no water and the horse nearly gone, all they'd ever found was that green dress in shreds and a few bones."

"Take me to a stage line, so I can get out of this country."

"I've got a better idea."

"What's that?" she asked, stretching her legs out.

"Have your own funeral."

"What? Are you crazy?" She frowned in bewilderment.

"If you're dead, I'll bet they'd stop looking for you. Pure and simple."

"Wait," she said shaking her head warily. "That is what I'm trying to avoid. Being dead."

"Let's say I take that crippled horse and the green dress back to New Field. Ask around about this girl I found dead up in the desert. We make a pile of rocks, say it's her grave."

"Where did you get this idea?" she asked.

"Oh, I just thought it up."

"I suppose you'd want me to stick around this place?" She shook her head vehemently. "No way, I could never stay here! This is too — too — I was raised on a damn farm."

"Suit yourself," he said, angry with her complete rejection of his plan. "You sleep in the tent on the cot. I'll sleep out here."

"It's not that I'm not grateful for all you —"

"Forget it!" he cut in sharply.

He shook his head as she stalked off to the tent. Stupid for him to even worry about her. In a day or two she'd be gone and out of his life. Why even fret about her? So what if some killers wanted to murder her? He had other worries.

THREE

A woman's shrill scream filled the night. Vince rose on his elbow. He felt for his pistol — nothing. He chided himself as he rose, quickly pulling on his britches. From here on, he needed to be more careful and sleep with his damn Colt, especially with the risk of her pursuers.

"What's wrong?" he shouted.

"There's a — a — rattlesnake in here!"

In the dim predawn light, he searched about for the ax. He grabbed the handle and hurried for the tent. From the flap, he could see her huddled on the far end of the cot. The unmistakable dry rasp of the sidewinder was inside the dark edge of the tent.

"Did he bite you?" he asked.

"No-o."

He swung the ax and felt the muscled body of the snake withering. Vince raked the serpent outside and finished cleaving off its head. Relieved the episode was over, he straightened.

She rushed out. Flinging herself at Vince, she hugged him for security. Wearing only the long tail shirt, she pressed her subtle body against him. When he reached to console her, she winced in pain from the sunburn. He withdrew his hand, feeling helpless to comfort her considering her sore skin. Still trembling she squeezed him harder.

"It's all over," he said to reassure her.

"It could have killed me!"

"This is the first time in a long time one's been in the camp. Sorry it came into the tent." Her soft, feminine body pressed against his began to awaken feelings he preferred to forget.

She finally released him and shook her head. "I'm sorry to be such a baby. But I knew a working girl once that got bitten and died. It was not a pretty sight."

"I'll make some coffee," he said, anxious to escape the desires her closeness kindled in him. He busied himself chopping tree limbs with a vengeance and soon had the fire going. Despite the cool predawn air, he found himself sweating. Then while he watched the long shadows emerge, the gentle east wind chilled him as the sun's first rays pinpointed the camp.

"I owe you a favor," she said softly, seated on the ground and tugging the shirt tail over her bare knees.

He shook his head to dismiss her gratitude.

"Sidewinders and other snakes come to this water." Wary of her power of attraction, he tried not to look at her. Her presence had become a physical thing that he tried hard to suppress. She'd be gone in a day or so, he reminded himself over and over. She's not the woman you've been imagining to stay and ranch with you. He needed to do something —

"The reason I was awake and heard the snake, I was thinking on this funeral plan of yours." Her voice grew louder and rang with impatience. "Well, what do you want from me?"

"I don't understand."

"Come on, the price? Everyone gets their cut."

"I hadn't set one — yet." He fumbled with his cigarette papers that wouldn't separate between his fingers. He was ready to stuff them back in his shirt pocket when she took them from him.

Deftly, she peeled a sheet off and took the pouch from his shirt pocket, loaded the V of paper with tobacco and rolled it up, sealing it with the tip of her tongue. She stuck the end in his mouth and grinned at him.

"You've been away from a woman too long." With a shake of her head as if amused, she turned and headed for the tent.

He took the paper cylinder out of his mouth, looked at it and then at her retreat. She probably was right. Way too long. He returned it to his lips, struck a match on the seat of his pants, and stared at the closed tent flaps. Finally he lighted the end and drew the smoke in deep.

In a short while, she reappeared wearing the shirt and cuffed up jeans with only her bare toes sticking out.

In near silence, they ate the reheated beans for breakfast. The coffee tasted a little weak to him but she never complained.

She finally broke the rift, standing above him holding her tin plate and spoon. "If you do this funeral business, what must I do? Stay here and be Missus . . . what?"

"Wagner," he said, looking up at her.

"Oh, yes. But even as Missus Wagner, how can I hide here?"

"Probably have to cut your hair short. You get a tan on that face instead of makeup, you might even look like Missus Wagner." He laughed aloud, amused at his reconstruction plans for her. He knew she'd never go through with the scheme anyway.

"I suppose I could take Sally or Phyllis for a new name too?"

"Whoever you'd like to be," he said, rising with the canvas pail in his hand.

"Wait. Don't leave yet. Do you think it will work?"

He looked her in the eye and nodded. Then went on to the pens to catch the horses. Her bay caught up easy, but the dun acted spooked and Vince made ready to rope him.

"Here," she said from behind him, slipping into the corral. "I'll catch him. He likes me."

"They need watered," Vince said, almost disgusted when the dun submitted to her putting a loop over his head. "When you get back, we'll feed them a little corn."

"Is the big black horse that's coming in yours too?" She motioned to the saddle stock ambling in for a drink at the tank.

Vince let the gate bars down for her and then headed for the feed box. From it, he scooped up corn to feed the big black horse in a small box on the ground. With pride of ownership, he currycombed the dust from the horse's coat. This was his catch horse when he rounded up mustangs and few men

44

owned better mounts. When she returned, he indicated the nosebags he'd put corn in for the other two horses.

After the horses were cared for, Vince busied himself in preparation to cut out her squaw boots. The leather laid out, he split out several long thin strips of the hide to use for lacing. The horses crunching hard corn nearby, she presented her foot on the piece he intended to use for the bottom. Her sole outlined, he handed her the lacing.

"Chew on these. It'll make them softer."

"Are you serious?" She wrinkled her nose in disbelief at his request.

"Yes."

Reluctantly she began to feed the lacing into her mouth, making distasteful faces at him. He remained solemn though inside he laughed at her reaction. She could stand a little more humbling just to be around.

"Where did that steamer trunk come from?" she asked, meaning the one in the tent.

"Found it along the road. The cot too. Even that chair."

"You kinda live on find-me-nots, don't you?"

"I guess."

"You've even found a wife out there."

"A what?" He blinked at her.

45

"Me. You've gathered up all this stuff in the desert and now you have me." She pointed at herself.

"Has me got a name?" he asked, amused at her analogy. Without looking up at her, he punched holes for the cord to lace the sides of the boots to the bottoms.

"No, I'm thinking, Stella, Donna, or Bonnie for sunbonnet."

"How about Dora?" Her new attitude was lots better.

"No." Half gagged sounding, she pulled the rawhide out of her mouth. "This tastes awful."

"Keep chewing on it," he said.

"These better be great boots," she mumbled, making a face at him.

Mid-morning, she was stomping her foot in her right one. The new footwear had piqued her curiosity. "This one feels very good."

"Here's the other one." He stood up to get the kinks out of his legs and back, then stretched his shoulders to drive out the stiffness from sitting so long. "Go catch the dun, he needs more riding anyway. Then gather your personal things. We're going to salt the trail."

"Salt the trail?" She frowned, a questioning light in her blue eyes.

"Yes. Scatter those button-up shoes, leave a few pieces of dress material on the way. And fix up a grave."

"Sounds like a lot of work," she said, then shrugged. In her new boots, she ran off light-footed to capture the dun.

Vince smiled after her. She probably would never stay. . . .

First, he salted the trail with one of her button up shoes he tossed beside a big boulder. Then he tore some of the dress material and latched it on the fishhook barbs of a barrel cactus beside the game trail. She agreed it looked very natural, as if she'd brushed against it and became entangled.

They worked into late afternoon to pile high the rocks that would make her cairn. Satisfied that the stack would cover a human body, Vince stepped back and, drawing a deep breath, wiped his sweaty face on his sleeve.

"Funerals are always sad." She mopped perspiration off her eyes and face with his kerchief.

He agreed with a nod.

"I've been thinking," she said hesitantly. "Maybe we won't have to cut my hair."

"It's part of the old you," he reminded her. She must be having regrets about losing her curls. He'd have to convince her. Vince went to catch the dun. Tied on a long lariat to graze while they worked, the gelding was easy to catch, otherwise he would have sent her. He returned with the horse.

"We can think about cutting my hair, can't we?" she asked.

"Depends on how complete you want your death to be. I say anyone ever saw you with that long hair would remember you." He mounted the dun and put his arm down for her.

"I know, keep my new boots out of his flank," she said as he swung her in place. "Oh, Vince, I surely will cry when you cut it."

"Me cut it?" he asked absently, busy studying the fiery sunset.

"Well, I sure can't see to cut it." She scooted up on the saddle behind him and hugged him. "Say an amen for Julie Dailey, she died today. We buried her under a pile of black stones." The side of her face rested on his back as she talked. "Her remains are planted on Jackass Flats. Is that really the name of this place?"

"I call it that because of the burros that hang out around here. In two days, they'll have wiped out all our signs."

A coyote wailed close to them. She started

and held him tighter.

"Is he very close?" she asked, her voice fluttering a bit.

"He won't hurt you."

"Are you sure? I've never been this close to one before. Let's get back to your place. He gives me goose bumps."

Vince let the dun have his head. The horse acted better. Either she'd had a calming effect on the animal, or he finally decided to give up his foolishness. But either way he was proud of the gelding. Also her arms seemed to be natural wrapped around him. He needed to remember not to put too much stock in her intimacies toward him. That was just her way of life.

Bone tired, they ate peppery dried jerky and washed it down with coffee. In the flickering firelight, they finished and smiled at each other.

"It tasted better than shoe lacing," she finally commented.

Vince knew what he must tell her next. There was no easy way to broach the subject.

"If you're through, we'll work on your hair."

"I wanted — you don't think?" She waited for an answer he wouldn't give. A reprieve from the shearing. Finally she relented.

"Never mind, you're probably right."

"I'll go get my things," he said, discovering as he stood up that the rock piling effort had stiffened his back.

In a few moments he returned with a candle reflector lamp, a sheet, and his straight edge razor. He set the small lamp on the chair so he would have enough light to see by. When he struck a match to the candle, the reflection shown on her face. He saw the tear run down her cheek as he got on his knees beside her.

"You just be careful," she sniffed. "I saw a girl get her throat cut with one of those one time."

Gingerly he lifted the long springy curl. He almost shut his own eyes as he severed her hair above the collar of her shirt. One by one he sliced away the buoyant locks.

He noticed as the hair piled on the ground around her how tightly she clenched her eyes. Vince had little doubt her fists matched them beneath the sheet.

"When I'm done I've got some soap to wash your head with."

"Lye soap?"

"No," he said, feeling sentimental as the end of his barbering drew near. "This is from the yucca root. I'm about through. Do you want to look at yourself in the mirror?"

50

"No!"

"This isn't your real funeral," he reminded her.

"Well, it feels like it is now. All day I doubted it. But now it really seems like it."

"Come on." He stood, frisked the sheet off her, and shook the hair into the fire to get rid of the evidence. "Let's go wash the rest down at the tank."

Stars shone on the still, dark mirror surface of the tank. With her kneeling beside the water's edge in the small circle of lamplight, he doused her head with a pail of water.

"Oh. That's cold." She shivered.

He smiled down at her and began working the yucca soap into her hair. The rich lather began to build under his fingers.

"That's good soap," she said as he worked his hands through the suds and her slick hair.

"Apache women use it," he said.

"You ever have one of them for your own squaw?" she asked.

"No." He chuckled. *You,* he said to himself silently, *are my first woman to almost own.* He rinsed her head twice with pails of water and then handed her the worn cotton towel.

"I've decided on a name," she announced, rising and toweling her hair. "May for maybe this will work."

He blew out the lamp. There were plenty of stars overhead to see their way back.

"May, huh? Well, May, tomorrow you can earn your keep. We'll go catch some mustangs. I need some more to break."

"Really?" she asked, threading her arm in his. "Can I really help you?"

He stopped under the canvas shade. "Yes, and you better get some sleep. It'll be another long day tomorrow."

"Good night, Vince," she said, almost sounding as if she actually regretted their parting.

"Night, May," he said after her.

He stood for a long time and stared at the tent. Were his hopes too high concerning her? He shook his head to clear his thoughts. She wasn't easily forgotten. Besides, he needed to gather some new mustangs.

FOUR

Beneath the frayed brim of the gray hat, dust streaked her face. Stirrup by stirrup with him, nothing could hide the enthusiasm in her blue eyes. Vince winked at her. Pride filled, he recounted. In five days they had captured that many stout young horses. What an awesome team they'd become in less than a week. Her tomboy riding impressed him.

"There." She pointed toward the mustang herd they surveyed. "Isn't that the bald-face two-year-old we missed capturing two days ago?"

He nodded as he studied the small band grazing below on the flat that separated them from the rushing Rio Verde with rows of tall cottonwoods on its sandy banks. The white-faced horse was obviously the best individual in the group.

"You head them this way," he directed. "I'll slip in and we'll capture him today."

"Yes," she said and pounded Vince on the leg with her fist. Hardly able to contain her excitement, she swung the dun horse to the right as they parted.

He shook his head a little in awe of the new her. May certainly had changed in the past few days. Apprehensive still, he turned the black horse northward to intercept the wild one when she began the drive.

The big horse slid down the hillside, sensing what was happening. Vince's saddle leather creaked from the powerful muscles of the black gathered beneath him. He shook his lariat loose. This colt would be valuable. With his color and carriage, once Vince broke him out, he could bring as high as fifty dollars.

Her wa-hoo carried up the long valley. The mustangs jerked their heads up, and with an eye on her as she drove them down the flats, they avoided seeing Vince and the black until he pressed within a few hundred yards. Too late. The colt was no match for the ground-gathering black. His neck stretched, hooves thundering, the black carried Vince closer and closer to the mahogany-colored colt laboring to outrun them.

The air whistled as the loop flew, then settled around the horse's neck. Vince eased down in the saddle, slowing the black so they did not break the wild one's neck the first time. Busy shortening the length of the rope, he dallied and re-dallied the rope around the horn while moving in closer.

"You've got him," she said.

She rode in from the side, shaking loose a rope to catch him. Did she have the skills to do that?

"Watch him when you rope him, he's a stout horse."

Her first loop fell short of catching him and made the horse spook and buck in protest, while he crowded the black in to shorten his rope some more.

"There," she shouted, her noose falling in place over his head. Determination tightened her facial muscles as she struggled to shorten the lariat. "We've really got him now."

"Be careful," he warned her as the mustang tried to show his heels and kick at them.

The stout young horse's nostrils flared as he breathed with a restriction from the ropes tight around his throat. The horse had to learn to stop fighting the constricting ropes. Still, fear of the pair of riders caused him to shy from both mounts and riders. Vince spooked him to make him move between them and to head for the corral in a lope.

Fresh faced and proud, leaned over the horn and working her side of the lead on the run, she shouted, "This could really get in your blood."

"I think it has," he said quietly.

With the hat cast aside on a string under her chin and riding mostly on her shoulders, her face had freckled in the sun. Even her short hair had lightened to a honey color. Her blue eyes gleamed as she hard rode across from him. First they'd caught a grulla-colored horse, then a blue roan filly, then two bays, a sorrel, and the last one was the bald-face horse they'd captured in the week on the Verde River. He had two months' horse training ahead to put into these individuals.

On horseback, looking over the captured horses in the pen at last, she smiled.

"Can I have Baldy to ride?"

"What about the dun?"

"I'd like something flashy. There isn't much of that in my life." She laughed.

"Do you miss it?" How much longer could she stand the dust and cactus spines before she fled him?

With a pensive look on her face she asked,

"How long have I been eating your beef jerky?"

"Close to a week up here."

"I really miss the good meals. I don't miss the hassles in the business. Nor the fights or the drunks. I don't miss being afraid. Or beat up. Some men are mean to you."

"Sorry I asked." He stepped out of the saddle. All the new horses were in the far end of the pen. Attached to each one was a rope with a good size log for them to drag around. He worked the new horse in the narrow chute, took off the lariat, and fixed a rope on him that wouldn't choke him and had its own log on the end of it. The rope and log were situated so they didn't get hung up when Vince let him out of the chute.

Baldy broke forward and soon learned he was not alone or free. He watched the horse's reaction and then, satisfied, began coiling both ropes.

There were some riders crossing by the river that caught his eye. Ropes on his saddle horn, he took the Colt out of his saddlebags and shoved it in his waistband. The arrivals were mostly hatless. That meant they were Indians.

She must have noted them too. "Who are they?"

"Keep hold of our horses. I can handle them."

"Whatever you say. Be careful, please."

He nodded. The intruders' arrival had upset her. She blanched and she hid behind the horses.

"They're friendly. Stay here." He knew them, and they had already seen her. They were good Indians.

"Hello, Horseman," the round-faced leader said, leaning heavily on the Spanish saddle horn. Horseman was the name the Papagoes had given him.

"Hello, Chief." Then he nodded at the other two.

"You catch lots of horses here?" the thickset Papago Chief, John Mendoza, asked.

"A few." Vince hated to brag. "Are you here to buy some horses?"

The chief shook his head.

"We search for Apaches," the leader said. "The army pays us for their heads. The Army only pays us for them. We go back."

"Well that's good news to me." The Papagoes were viewing his new horses.

"You find woman, Horseman?" The chief laughed loud. "She plenty good help to gather horses with."

Mendoza said something in his own language and the other two bucks laughed with him. Vince knew it was over her. The men were more interested in her but tried to act as if the mustangs were worthwhile.

"You want to buy some of my good horses?" he asked them.

"Sell me the black horse?" Mendoza grinned.

Vince shook his head at that offer. "Spend your army money, these are good."

"Papagos are horse poor." The chief laughed, shook his head still amused.

"Now Horseman will have many children. You have big time, *amigo.* New wife for you, good thing." They prepared to leave.

"Ride home easy," he said after them.

They saluted him in Spanish and then headed southwest through the towering armed saguaros to cross the big saddle mountain. He turned to face an ashen-faced May.

"Are — are they gone?"

He shook his head to dismiss her concern. "They were just some Papagos."

"When I saw you get out that gun, I just knew we were dead."

He pulled her in his arms and hugged her. "They are simply scouts for the army, looking for signs of Apaches."

"Are there Apaches around here?" she asked.

"You want me to lie to you?"

"No." She released him and turned on her heel to pace back and forth between him and the pen. "Let's go home right now." She rolled her lip in and out under her upper teeth.

"Tomorrow," he said.

"No, Cowboy. I couldn't sleep a wink here thinking there were Apaches around me."

"Leaving now is plumb crazy with a half dozen green horses and miles of cholla and spiny cactus to fight. No."

About to cry, she said, "Oh, I saw three men that they killed."

"Quit worrying. Apaches come and go. They never bothered anything I own." He gathered her in his arms to assure her. But he realized some deeper rooted force was involved than the Indian threat when she looked up at him.

In a moment of truth, he bent his face down to her posed lips. Then he tasted a growing sweetness that desert honey could never match. Her arms sought his neck and desperately they began searching with their mouths for those deeper answers. They couldn't get enough of each other, slowly sinking to their knees as the passion consumed them.

He wanted to carry her to their bedrolls, but he feared his move might break the spell. At last dazzled with her, he swept her up, rose, and delivered her to the blankets for a bed.

Her breath came in great gulps as they began to undress each other. In the process, his cramped fingers pushed aside her shirt, revealing the peeled shoulders. He doubted his hands would ever be the same. The paleness of her skin beyond the sunburn line frightened him as something sacred he shouldn't have exposed. Yet he realized that she shared his wish for them to be one as well. Words for him were insignificant as they fought to be one with headstrong determination.

The shock of their bodies meshed in fury was soon spent. Afterwards, neither said a word, afraid to speak, fearful a single word might spoil the magic they'd felt. From time to time they kissed each other impulsively on the mouth.

Wordless, he led her by the hand to the rushing river. Seated in the stream, with her on his lap, the cool water flowed past barely halfway up his chest while he savored her soft body. Overhead the star-flecked sky appeared to him to be closer than ever before.

FIVE

Tied on the back of his saddle, the coffee pot clanked like a bell. Vince led four proud mustangs off with the black horse. He turned and smiled at May as she handled the other three wild ones from her dun. In the soft morning light, they crossed the wide pass between the red granite mountain and the black slopes. The trail through the giant saguaros was a well-defined route as they climbed out of the valley of the Verde and into the great basin beyond.

Midday, they paused under the shade of an ironwood tree at a small water source. The mustangs were still too wild and wouldn't take water from the pail, so they went without a drink. The saddle stock watered, he sat beside her as she hugged her knees to study the distant sweep of the desert. She'd said little since they left the Verde. He wondered what was wrong.

"You all right?" he asked, handing her the

canteen.

She nodded and took a swallow. "I don't think I'm cut out to do this." She gave a great sigh. "And another thing — I wasn't going to get involved with you."

"Was it that bad?" He studied her face for the answer.

"No." She averted her face.

"Then what was wrong?"

"I'm not certain. I've never done that before."

He frowned at her in disbelief. "Done what, May?"

"Oh." She drew a deep breath, "I'm no little innocent. But last night scared me."

"How?" Vince couldn't imagine what she was trying to say.

"You! This is all stupid. I wasn't going to get involved with you and your two-bit outfit. I hate buzzards circling me and snakes in my tent and a damn scorpion in my blankets. I want silk dresses and a house with a floor and a roof and servants."

"We'll be back to camp in a few hours. You'll feel better then," he assured her. Then he struggled to his feet and went to get ready to move on. "I can take you to catch the stage."

"Vince?" she called out. "I'm sorry. I did like chasing mustangs and yes, you . . . can't you see it would never work, me staying here?"

He nodded that he'd heard her. But her words didn't elevate his mood. Just when he thought things would go better, she changed her mind. Her staying with him was too much to bank on. Frustrated with the knowledge, he handed her the leads to the three wide-eyed colts

Back at Cottonwood Springs, he plain busied himself haltering the mustangs and tying blocks to their drag ropes while May scurried about unloading their camp goods. Then he stripped the bridle off the black and patted him on the neck. When he undid the dun's head stall, he felt she was watching him closely.

"You just turning him loose?" she asked, concerned.

"Sure, he's a woman's horse, he'll stay close."

"We need some water." She handed him the pail. Then a smile spread across her face. "Don't get all the water. We'll need to take a bath together after sundown won't we?"

Together? That did sound interesting. Had she told him something or was it simply a slip of her tongue? He'd see later.

The next morning, he tried to concentrate

on the blue roan filly. He could hardly shake the bath business from the night before. He snubbed the horse close to the post in the center of the pen, then waved the saddle blanket at her. The filly snorted at him, her eyes wide.

Softly, he began speaking to ease her fears. Another step closer. The mustang furiously shook her head to try to escape the heavy halter restraining her.

"Vince!" May called from behind him.

"What is it? I'm busy," he said, not looking back at her. This filly was about to learn about man.

"There's two riders coming from the west."

He paused and dropped the blanket. Who the hell was coming? He stripped off his gloves. "Did they see you?"

"I don't think so." Her face flushed as she spoke.

"Get in the tent and stay there. I'll handle them."

He left the filly and eased himself between the bars of the gate, then stood on his toes. He still couldn't see anyone. From the saddlebags, he secured the Colt, grateful May was out of sight in the tent. He stuck the .44 in his waistband and squatted to pour a cup of coffee. Ever mindful, he heard the approach of the horses' hooves clacking on rocks in the wash.

Both riders wore bowlers and their once-white shirts were soaked in sweat, their horses lathered. Rising to face them, Vince recognized the hard look they bore on their faces. The garters on their sleeves indicated they were hired guns.

The red-bearded one rode his horse up in front of Vince. The other *hombre* stopped short.

"Howdy," the bearded one offered.

Vince acknowledged them with a nod. They weren't there for social etiquette. Neither man probably had a manner left in him that didn't serve his own purpose.

"We need a little information about a grave west of here. You know anything about who's buried out there?" He jerked his thumb over his shoulder for the direction.

"I didn't know her," Vince said, still sizing up the pair.

"Did you talk to her?"

Vince shook his head. "She'd been dead a day, maybe longer, when I saw the buzzards. Some dance hall girl in a green dress. Couldn't tell how she died. She might have run out of water and got lost or snake bit."

"You find any money on her?"

"No, why?" He frowned as he waited for

their explanation.

"She stole a lot of money from her former employer," the bearded man said.

"Well, she must have spent it before she got to Jackass Flats." Vince chuckled.

"What's so damn funny?" the second one demanded.

"Nothing. Boys, she didn't even have a purse with her when I found her body." Vince said. "Her crippled horse is out in the corral. Must have thrown a shoe. Bad shape, still limps, you want it?"

"No," the second rider said, pushing in closer. "You look familiar to me, mister."

"Vince Wagner, that's my name."

"No." The man shook his head and backed his horse. "I guess you just look like someone I used to know."

The bearded one gave his partner a disapproving head shake and turned back to him. "That's all we needed."

Vince stood his ground, waiting to be sure they didn't try something. He eased some when they turned their mounts and headed back. Obviously stiff from being in the saddle so long, they were uncomfortable and unaccustomed to so much riding. He drew a deep settling breath and slowly exhaled, then turned on his heel and headed for the tent.

"Are they gone?" May asked from inside.

"Stay put," he said flatly. "They're hired guns and I don't trust them."

"The clean shaven one is Frank Dean," she explained. "The one with the red beard is Harty Mills. They're Allison's killers."

"Dean, Denton, or Dimer," Vince said. "He's using a different name then when I met him before."

"You knew him?" she asked, shocked by the knowledge.

"It was a long time ago."

"Did he recognize you?"

"Maybe."

"Vince, they're a bunch of damn liars. I never took a gawdamn stinking penny from Allison. Cripes!"

"Take it easy. I believe you." He smiled. "Keep out of sight. They'll probably circle around and check us out."

"Who are you, Vince Wagner?" she asked point blank.

"You said it."

"No." She shook her head. "Here I've been worried you were the nice guy, that I was some kinda trash and you —"

"I've never lied to you," he said.

"It's all an act isn't it? Who you really are?"

"May, come dark, I'm going to take you up on the mountain in case." He shook his head. "I figure they'll come back tonight to check this place out. They ain't fools."

"Answer my question," she demanded. "Who are you?"

"We can hash that later. We've got to convince them that you're dead."

"Do you believe I didn't steal that money?"

"Yes. Now we have a choice. We can either kill them or let them go back and tell Allison that you are dead, right?"

She made a small nod.

"If that fails, we have two choices then, kill, or be killed, huh?" He hugged her shoulder to comfort her, but stormed his brain for an idea for their defense.

After sunset, he led May by the hand around the corral. Bedroll tucked under his arm, he paused to pick up a rawhide riata from the corral. He stopped once to see if anything was moving out in the basin under the starlight. Nothing he could see, but his guts warned him the pair was still out there. He guided the way up the steep slope around the towering saguaros and the silver cholla with its glistening thin needles.

"There's a small flat up here where you can stay until just before dawn. I'll come back and get you if they haven't shown up."

"Are there snakes up here?" she asked.

"I'll make a circle around you with the riata. A snake won't cross it," he said softly, listening to the night sounds.

"Are you sure?" she asked, squeezing his arm as they halted to catch their breath.

"Yes. Believe me."

"I do. I'm just upset that those gun-toting bastards found us."

"It could be perfect. We'll resolve your death once and for all."

She gave a sigh. "Do you really think they're out there?"

"Yes. Now if anything happens to me, you slip down and ride the dun south. Hear me?" He waited for her reply. The business at hand had turned serious and he wanted a straight answer from her.

"Anything happens to you?" she asked, bewildered. "You are going to be careful?"

"You just remember to ride south if anything goes wrong."

"I will."

He found the flat was devoid of all but the bristle of spring grasses gone dry. He spread her blankets, then laid down the riata as a perimeter guard.

"Vince?" she called softly as he straightened. "Kiss me."

He stepped into the ring. There were times she acted so damn tough and other times so vulnerable. He took her face in his rough calloused palms and pressed his lips to hers. Slowly he released her. "Sleep well, Missus Wagner."

"You . . . be careful, Mister Wagner."

He backed away and adjusted the pistol in his waistband. Careful not to dislodge a rock or make a loud noise, he descended the mountain. There was no sign of any movement in the starlit greasewood land beyond. Far away, a coyote broke the stillness. Would she panic alone by herself up there? He hoped she wouldn't scare easy.

At the corral he checked on the mustangs. They acted snorty and moved about restlessly as if they knew more than he did. Maybe he was just on edge. Indian-like he crept around the pens. He found a place to sit cross-legged. With the .44 in his lap, he waited.

Ashes from the fire glowed red when the gentle night wind touched them. His back against the pole, he waited. Just the sizzle of the night insects and occasional snort from a mustang broke the silence.

"See anything, Dean?" a stage whisper came in the darkness.

At once he became wide awake at the gunman's words. His muscles tensed as he filled his hand with the Colt's grip. He strained to hear them and their location.

"No. Hush," Dean said.

"You figure the girl's here?"

"I think she's dead. We got to be sure he don't talk. She might have told him before she died. Besides I know that dude from somewhere."

"Where?"

"Shut up."

Statue-like, he watched their outlines as they crept up to the tent. Their bent-over silhouettes blended with the night shadows. But the dull sheen from their gun barrels gave their positions away. Ear shattering reports of their pistols broke the night, and the orange blasts flared as they shot up his bed in the tent.

"Is she in there?"

"He ain't moving, by Gawd."

"Don't either of you move a damn hair!" Vince ordered.

Their pistols flashed in response to his orders. They swore at him as they wildly shot into the night. Hammers clicked on empty cylinders and, cursing, they ran pell-mell out of his camp. Vince's shots after them were deliberately high. A smile crossed his face as he heard them in the dry wash, cussing their horses. He rose and reloaded the Colt as the sound of their retreating hooves waned off in the night. Damn their worthless hides, they didn't need to stop till they got back to New Field. Satisfied the threat was over, he hiked past the corral and back up the mountain.

As he drew near, May began calling out softly in the night. "Is that you, Vince?"

"Yes, it's over. They're gone."

"Thank God. Did it work?"

"I imagine so. But we'll stay up here tonight just in case."

"Yes," she said softly as he lay down beside her. Her hungry mouth found his and smothered him. He wondered how she would act about this lovemaking in the morning.

Six

"I'll be back in two days," Vince promised as he finished tying on his bedroll. "You keep an eye out, but I'm satisfied those two hired killers never stopped this side of New Field."

"I could take a horse and ride out of here," she said with a threat in her voice.

"It's a free country." He paused to stare after as she walked to the corral and studied the mountain with her back to him. For his part he hoped she didn't do anything foolish.

"Oh I'll be here," she finally admitted and turned with a grin. "Get going before I change my mind."

Earlier they'd discussed her accompanying him and decided the less exposure she had to others in the basin, the less suspicion and gossip there would be. And where she came from could be kept from outsiders. Ready to go, he picked up the lead to the four broke horses and headed south. In two days and one night and he'd back with her. He set out in a long lope with his string of mustangs trailing him. He already missed her.

Late in the afternoon, with the horses delivered and the money in his vest pocket, he swung by Pick Walters's store far ahead of his original schedule. A short, weathered, wooden-frame windmill squeaked in protest to the hot wind, issuing a slender stream out of the pipe into the masonry tank. His throat parched, he drank from the spout to cool his mouth.

"Don't drink it all, cowboy," a voice behind him ordered.

Vince rose up, the cool water still dripping off his chin. "You still charging regular customers for a drink?"

"Not regular customers, but you don't come by often to be classed as one of them." Pick stood bare-headed in the doorway. A thin man in his thirties, wearing a clean white shirt and gold-rimmed glasses, he leaned one shoulder against the door facing. "Put that horse up, Vince, and come in here, I've got a bottle and can't seem to find enough folks to help get it emptied."

His horse in the corral, Vince brushed some of the road dust from his clothing as he walked to the store. Inside, he spotted Pick and joined him. They took seats at the table in the center of the cluttered store that smelled of dry goods, Mexican spices, and leather oil.

"You must have sold some mustangs." Pick poured whiskey into the tin cup before Vince.

"Brought Tom Watson four head."

"Damn! A man flush with money. Could I sell you this store?" Pick waved his arm around to indicate all the merchandise.

Vince shook his head. Walker had a good sense of humor. The whiskey cut the dust caked on his teeth.

"It's too good to sell to the Indians ain't it?" Pick said.

"Way too good to do that."

"*Amigo,* a couple days ago a pair of hard cases came by here looking for a dance hall girl." Pick's dark eyes centered on him. "I ain't seen them since."

"I seen them. Sent them packing. They tried to bushwhack me."

Pick shook his head. "They looked the part. Tough pair. What in hell were they doing looking for a dance hall gal up here?"

"She rode up there," Vince said, wondering if she'd stopped at the store. He'd heard her mention a rundown store. Strange. He'd always figured it was Walters's. "I found her after the buzzards did. Buried her up on Jackass Fiats."

"Was she pretty?" Pick asked.

"Guess she had been," Vince said, like he didn't want to discuss the remains.

"Army's got those Papagos out scouting for the Apaches." Pick shook his head in disgust. "You figure they could even find an Apache's tracks?"

"Probably." Had the chief or one of his bunch told Pick about his woman? One damn lie led to another.

He grimaced to himself.

"I spoke to some the other day," Vince said, waiting to see if Pick knew about May.

But instead the man stood up, poured more whiskey in Vince's cup, and sat back down. "I've wanted to just sell this place and go somewhere it's green and the rivers run neck deep."

"You need to lock up and go get a couple nights of lucky charm with some parlor woman," Vince suggested.

"Would you go with me?" Pick raised his eyebrows.

"I sure would." He lied to humor his friend. "But I've got a pen full of mustangs to get back to."

77

"Damn, she was dead when you found her."

Vince nodded. He'd had enough whiskey. Any more and he might get his stories twisted. He owed her his allegiance, since he'd made up her death. Besides, he found being away from her left something out of his life.

"Say, Pick, I need a few things before I head back to my place. Those ponies will need water by the time I get there."

"Aw, stay the night. I've still got plenty of this whiskey." He held up the amber bottle against the light to measure it. "Those two rannies told me that she stole a lot of money from her ex-boss."

"They told me that too. But she must have spent or lost it before I found her. She was sunburned to a crisp, had a rag of a green dress barely covered her."

"Did you look around for the money?"

Vince shook his head. "Hell, if she'd had money, she'da took a stage and got the hell away, not rode some crippled horse off the main road in a silk dress." He shook his head to emphasize his point.

Pick laughed. "You're right! She'd never got herself lost up there." He removed his eyeglasses as if to check the lens. "You know, those damn Apaches could come

78

back any time. They used to water at your place for years. I damn sure wouldn't stay up there."

"I figure they don't want me," Vince said. "I've been there three years now."

"What do you need?" Pick hooked his gold frames behind his ears.

"Beans, corn meal, coffee, dried apples, brown sugar if you have any, and some hemp rope."

"You're still catching a lot of mustangs?" Pick got busy filling the order.

"Some, but I want to go into the high country. There may be some good ones running up there."

"You're braver than I am. I wouldn't sleep a night out there where you are or go higher for all the damn horses in the world."

"How much is that slicker up there?" he asked, thinking of May.

"A dollar."

"Mine got tore, I'll take it too."

The items on the counter, Pick licked the stubby lead pencil and added up the figures on a piece of brown paper. "You want a bottle of that trading whiskey?"

"How much?"

"Three dollars, and I ain't making any money on it."

May might like it. He hated to waste

money, but he didn't dare buy any yard goods for her. "Sure, put it in."

"Your bill comes to seven dollars with the whiskey." Pick looked up expectantly.

Vince paid him. The storekeeper put the purchases in a cotton poke.

"You be careful. Them red heathens murdered two men up by Globe just three weeks ago. They were camped out and taking some horses to a man." Pick shook his head. "I wish you'd move closer to me. We could watch out together for them murdering devils."

The sun was setting as Vince saddled the black. He slung the loop of the sack over his horn and tied the oilskin-smelling slicker on with his bedroll.

"You got plenty ammunition for that Spencer repeater?" Pick asked, noting the rifle in the boot.

"Oh, couple of tubes."

"You may need them. Those Apaches have gone mad. Sure wish you and me could go somewhere and dance with the old elephant. We'd do some parlor girls a big favor."

To be friendly, he agreed and mounted up. Just a few weeks before, he would have jumped at Pick's invite to go enjoy a night or two of pleasure at Maxie's fancy parlor house. But as he set the black northward for home, he smiled to himself. May was waiting for him. The notion warmed him more than any whiskey ever had. He waved goodbye to Pick and nudged the black into a lope.

With only the stars and a few coyotes for company, he crossed the great basin of silver greasewood and giant, shadowy cactus. Near the first gray light of dawn, he rode out of the dry wash and started up the grade to the camp. May, where are you? Probably asleep. He was back nearly a full day sooner than he'd promised her.

The black snorted wearily at the same moment Vince noticed the corral bars were down. She'd left him. He stepped off the horse.

No, she wouldn't just turn loose the mustangs they'd captured. The night wind cooling his face, he looked around. His hand gripped the wooden handle of his Colt. Something was amiss.

"May! Where are you?" he shouted, hurrying to the tent. The crawling in his gut became more intense. If anything had happened. . . .

The flap gently waved, telling him she was not there as he burst inside. The blankets were gone, the cot turned over, his trunk pilfered through. Her corset lay on the ground. Puzzled, he bent over and recovered it. A smell in the tent came to his nose for a moment. Not her sweet scent, but the earthy musk of campfire and raw meat.

Vince stumbled outside, numb with his discovery. The Apaches had taken his woman. How? Why? He drew the Colt, carefully scrutinizing the area.

At the fire pit, he dropped to his right knee and touched the ashes. They were cold. In the deep shadows of the rustling cottonwoods, he looked to the sun-gilded top of Hondo Mountain. Why had they taken her? She did them no harm. He closed his eyes.

Vince remounted the black. He would need some horses.

Hopefully the Apaches had managed to take only a few of the mustangs. They'd obviously been in a hurry when they abducted her. The loss gnawed at his belly like a hungry beaver topping a tree.

In an hour, he had gathered four of the mustangs whose trailing ropes had stopped them along with the dun. His suspicions were confirmed. The Indians had been in too big of a hurry to capture more of his stock. Apaches ate horses for sustenance, although they preferred a mule's sweet meat. Why let the horses loose and take only her?

He loaded a packsaddle on the dun, quickly shifted the foodstuffs he'd bought to the panniers. Then he added an ax and the new rope. He found three more tubes of bullets for the Spencer the Apaches had overlooked. The sun was well on the rise when he left his place with the mustangs and dun in tow. He'd included the white corset in his saddlebags.

Midday, he sloshed his train into the Verde crossing. Pausing in midstream, he allowed them to water. He twisted in the saddle to look around. No tracks to follow. From here on he'd have to rely on his knowledge of the Indians' usual movement and his own intuition. As he studied the towering purple peaks above him, he wondered if she was still alive. May's a survivor, he assured himself.

Across the river, he dismounted and cut a large sapling to use. He fashioned a staff, then laced half the corset to it as a flag of truce.

Hold on, gal, I'm coming.

Remounted, he shoved the base of the pole in his right boot and set the black horse into a lope. His banner flapping above his head and the horses in tow, he loped eastward.

The land he faced consisted of stairstep

ranges and broken canyons, a place folks called the Brakes. A land where the Mexicans had a few words for the area, something like Place of the Apaches. The Indians could hold off three armies and ambush anyone at will. Death awaited him.

In late afternoon, he camped on a mesa. Water trickled in the wash nearby to quench the saddle stocks' thirst. With a pile of stones for a base, he planted the flag of truce in the middle of his camp. Vince felt certain, as the red blasts of sundown emblazoned the towering peaks above him, the Indians were aware of his intrusion.

The Spencer rifle close beside him, he barely slept, listening to the night sounds. The Apaches hated the night, when the lost souls from their past roamed the land. Still, he found little rest. Even the horses seemed to sense some form of surveillance and shifted, grunting in their sleep.

At dawn he built a small fire and boiled coffee. Rolling a cigarette, he watched the flat area clad in scrub greasewood brush around him. Patience, Vince reminded himself. To outwait them, he needed the most restraint as the rising wind fluttered the corset on its pole.

He planned to water the horses later. Sunup was a time the Apaches usually stirred, like a lot of other desert creatures. He seated himself cross-legged on the ground, while the small pungent fire set the coffee to a rolling boil.

When the brave first appeared, Vince wondered if the man came by himself. Perhaps it was a trap. Wearing a red cloth headband, the Apache's long black hair bounced on his shoulders as he jogged effortlessly across the mesa. Vince drew a deep breath to steady his thrashing heartbeat.

Was this one alone? The bones were tossed, it was too late to regret his action. Either he would win or lose. Feeling edgy, he rose to greet the lone Apache.

"Horseman," the brave took a hard look at his camp.

Vince nodded and indicated the space across the small fire. "Sit, I have coffee."

"You are very determined." The man's English was better than Vince expected.

"Perhaps I'm foolish." Vince poured his guest a cup of the steaming brew. "I come to trade horses for my woman."

"She may not be alive."

Vince shook his head. "Oh, she is still alive or you would not have come today."

"At first we laughed at your flag. It made

no sense. But now we know. You are a brave man."

"I've come for her," Vince said, not anxious to just talk with this man.

"This woman has died before?" the man asked.

What did the Indians know of their scheme? If they thought May had supernatural powers, perhaps they would spare her. All Indians were very superstitious, and that flaw could work to his advantage.

"There is a grave for her," the Indian announced.

"Yes. This woman is not a spirit against Apaches," Vince said, "but she has much power with my people."

"Did you bring the Papagos?" The Apache looked very cross.

"No, I'm alone. I come to trade horses to the Apaches for my woman."

"We can kill the Papagos." He seemed to scoff at their threat. "We only let them ride about this place until we tire of them."

"I do not doubt the skill of your people. The Papagos are not aware I'm here. I've come for my woman."

A small smile creased his copper face. "You would make a good warrior."

"Who taught you English?"

"I was taken from my people as a boy. But

now I am where I should be, back with my people."

"This woman belongs to me."

The brave shook his head. "Perhaps my people think something else. They may want to kill you."

"Do the Apaches not honor that flag?" He pointed to the limp corset on the stick above them.

"They arrested the great Chiricahua leader Cochise under such a trick. They even shot our people with such lies."

"So the Apaches want to lie too?" Vince asked, fishing out the makings to roll himself a cigarette.

"You wish to smoke for peace?" the buck asked.

"I smoke to pass the time. The Apaches and I have long had peace." He'd had no trouble in the past with them.

"A few Tontos is all. They are squaw followers. The real people have no peace with the white man."

"Fine, then we are not friends. Trade me the woman back and I will leave your land."

"You are not afraid of the Apaches?" The man squinted in disbelief.

"A man's a fool not to fear his least enemy." Vince rose and passed the cigarette over to the brave. The Indian lighted it with a twig from the fire. Vince watched him. This man was not all Indian.

"Are you a chief?" Vince asked, building himself a smoke.

He shook his head. "My other name is Juan Lopez. My mother was a Jacarilla Apache, my father a Mexican. When I was twelve I ran away to join my people camped near Tucson. In town, I was neither white nor Indian. These people made me one of them. I am an Apache."

Vince understood. "Perhaps I am a spirit." He knew Indians were concerned about such things.

"No," Juan said shaking his head. "I have seen Jesus in the church."

He nodded. "You are wise in many ways."

"Tomorrow, I will return to trade with you or to kill you." The man rose to his feet.

Deep in his own thoughts, he stared at Indian's knee-high boots. Once more the bones were cast. His lot would be to fight them or trade for his woman.

He rose as he watched the Apache swiftly cross the flats and disappear. Disappointed, he shook his head. The horses needed to be watered and hobbled.

This day would pass slowly.

He had to prepare for the worst. Vince closed his eyes.

After he completed his other tasks, the large knife in his belt needed to be sharpened. The chore required hours. Seated on the ground, he listened to the quail's short calls and whetted the edge of the knife on a stone. He also worried about May and her treatment in their hands.

SEVEN

Dawn brightened the higher peaks and lanced yellow rays on the greasewood and cactus-cloaked hills. The three mustangs, plus the dun and the black, were picketed close by. He'd saddled the black earlier and threw his pack gear on the dun in preparation for either success or retreat.

The horses looked up and Vince followed their lead to view the pair who materialized coming through the greasewood, one man hatless, the other wearing a red headband. They both rode thin horses. As they drew closer, he saw the black paint streaks on their faces. Like a sledgehammer blow to his chest, his heart stopped before they reached the flat.

They'd come for war. Strange, Apaches were skilled hide-and-seek fighters. They wouldn't be so brazen as to ride up like this unless they considered him a weak enemy. Vince knew better — at least they'd come to talk first.

He rose slowly, arms folded across his chest. A topknotted quail whistled sharply in the chaparral. Was this a diversion to distract him? Where was May? The pair dismounted at a great distance.

"Horseman," Juan called from where they stood. "We've come to trade many horses for the woman."

Although a wave of relief spread over Vince, he reminded himself to maintain his guard — just in case.

"Good. Come into my camp."

The small man with Juan showed his age. Wrinkles creased his leathery face, but his eyes were diamond-cut black coal that missed nothing.

"This is Chato," Juan said.

"An honor," Vince said politely.

"You are a great horseman like they call you," the chief said.

Vince accepted the man's praise with a nod. "I have three horses to trade."

"The black one?" Juan asked.

"No, that is how I live. I use him to catch the others."

The two men spoke in their own dialect. Chato said something in Apache as if he were angered by Vince's refusal. Both men appeared upset at his denial to enter the black into the negotiations.

"Ask Chato how many horses he gave for his bride," Vince requested, hoping to distract their thoughts away from the black horse. He was prepared to kill or be killed, but the black was not, for the moment, the topic under discussion.

When Chato laughed out loud, Vince relaxed. The chief and Juan spoke to each other in Apache. They seemed to be very heated about something.

Juan finally turned to Vince. "He says you are a good trader. But you owe him four more horses besides these for the woman."

"I will catch them in a few weeks." Vince waited for their answer. Did they trust him? Would they keep May until he had the horses captured?

Vince watched the pair's reaction with intense scrutiny.

When Juan translated terms. Chato nodded in agreement.

"Chato says you are good man. She will join you soon," Juan said. "If you speak the truth and the Papagos are not on your heels, the woman will come to you."

"I brought no such —" Vince realized his meeting with the dried-up little chieftain and Juan had ended. They were preparing to leave him and take the three mustangs with them. "Wait! Where will I find her?"

Juan turned back. "She will come as a spirit on your way home." Then they mounted and left him, leading off the ransom he paid.

Spirit, my butt! That gal better be all right or I'll find their camp and have my own damn war with the red bastards.

He cinched up the girth and swung aboard the black. There was no sign of the Apaches or the horses they had taken. Had they lied to him?

He rode west. Ever alert to a trap or an ambush, he let the silky-maned black horse pick his own pace. Several times he rose in the stirrups and cast hard glances at the land around him. The big black descended from the Andalusian blood of Coronado's stables. Seldom did one so pure come from the wild ones. A previous owner who never saw the greatness in the horse had gelded the black, a fact Vince had lamented many times.

The seller in Tucson had spoken of Spain. But Vince was satisfied to own such an animal and his pedigree or source was unimportant. He counted himself lucky the Apaches had not simply killed him and taken the animals. Quality horses meant little to the red man except to ride or eat when they became hungry.

The tree line on the western horizon meant he was near the Verde. In late afternoon, he rode out of the Brakes. Still no sign of May. Above him the cottonwood leaves rustled and the Verde gurgled past in its race to the Salt. Disappointment clouded his thoughts as he forded the stream. He mounted the bank and shook his head. There was no sign of her around the corrals they'd used to hold the wild ones.

He dropped heavily to the ground. Where was she? Disgusted at his lack of success, he unsaddled the black. The concern over her whereabouts became a lead weight in his stomach. He checked the perimeter again, then turned the big horse loose, satisfied the animal would not wander far. Next, he unloaded the dun and hobbled him.

The sun was setting when he built the fire and hung the pot of water on for coffee. Too distraught to eat, he watched the flames and wondered where she was.

"Vince?"

Jarred to awareness, he wondered if his ears were deceiving him. He wanted so much to hear her, had he imagined her call? He listened hard. Above the river's rush, someone was definitely calling his name. Was it a trap? The Colt in his hand, he raced across the sandy ground for the river. Was she there?

"Vince!" she screamed.

In the twilight, he saw her scramble down the steep sandy bank on the far side. Suspicious at first, he searched for a sign of an ambush. But he was so anxious to be with her that his own desires soon overrode caution. He pushed into the river, never stopping. The Colt in his right hand, in midstream he wrapped his arms around her to gather her in relief. The cool water filled his boots as he held her against his body. Holding, hugging, kissing each other with a consuming need and relief filling them.

"I'm sorry," he told her as he half carried her over the slippery moss-covered bottom.

May buried her face in his shirt. "They grabbed me when I stepped out of the tent. I thought I was dead for sure. At first, I thought they wanted my body, but —" She gave a great shudder and hugged him tightly. "They seemed in a great hurry to go to the mountains. They rode like the devil was after them. Their camp is in a deep canyon. For some reason, after they got me there, they just ignored me. Juan spoke to me. He told me you would come."

"Did they —"

She gave a shudder and a long sigh. "I

95

think the boys who took me wanted to. But they were very young and in too big a hurry to stop even for that. At first, Juan said they would get the big black horse in trade for me."

"They might have. But I could see they would trade for less."

Still a little awed by her return, he considered his good fortune having her alive. But the fact a small raiding party of very young bucks took her explained a lot to him.

"Juan said you out-traded the chief."

"To mess with Chato is dangerous. I'm just glad you're all right. It is some kind of miracle you're unscathed."

"Vince? Would you have traded the black for me?"

"You're my responsibility." He sat on the ground and pulled off his wet boots. "Yes, if I had to."

"But how would you have ever run down mustangs?"

He looked at her as she hugged her jean-clad legs. "Maybe there would have been no need to do that without you."

She pressed her forehead against her knees. "Those Apaches have very little food. Only some ground corn mush."

"Are you hungry?" he asked.

"Yes, but I want to bathe first," she said.

"I feel so dirty."

"I'll cook some beans and bacon," he offered.

She tugged on his sleeve. "No, go with me. I'm afraid of the night. We can cook later. I want you there while I bathe."

He rose and looked down in her eyes. Somehow he would make this ordeal up to her. Some way.

EIGHT

"You never told me where you came from," she said, chewing on the long grass stem.

He looked up from shoeing the dun's hind foot. Was this the time to tell her about his past? Would she keep his secret? Vince drew a slow breath before he spoke. "I guess you got a right to know." He rapped in the new nails in the horse shoe.

"Vince Wagner tell me," she insisted. "Where'd you grow up?"

"I grew up in the south. My mother's folks owned a big Georgia plantation. My daddy liked to play cards and he must have been good at it. When the war came along, daddy and my Uncle Talburt signed up and left.

"When it was over and the South lost, they come home old men at thirty-five. Bitter, they hated blacks, whites, Yankees. Worse they hated themselves for losing the war. Defeat ain't pretty on the faces of men used to winning.

"We didn't have any help. Fields grew up in weeds. I was still a teenager. Mom and some of the blacks who stayed, we tried to farm with some worn-out old mules. Loose hogs kept breaking in our truck patches. I had to shoot them.

"Things were pretty desperate. I went to town for help. That's when I found Paw and my uncle. They were laying up in an old shack with some whores, dead drunk and smelling worse than hogs. I was so ashamed that I couldn't get them to help I went home and told mother they had died."

Vince busied himself driving the nails. He hadn't thought about those days in years.

"How did you get out here?" she asked.

He put his hands on his waist to straighten his back. In another day or two they'd be ready to head for the high country. He gave his head a shake and began.

"Next thing I knew, a carpetbagger served delinquent tax papers on my maw. We had no money to pay any tax. I saw the incident had broken her heart. I went to town and shot the man. He died like a boar hog I'd once killed, gurgling on his own blood. But they didn't take kindly to anyone gunning down Federal people, so I hightailed it to the Indian lands."

"What then?" She sat down on a nail keg

as he rasped down the next hoof.

"That winter, I denned up in an old cabin with a couple of guys. Not much to do. One of our bunch, a boy my age, took pneumonia. His name was Steerman. We looked a lot alike, blond hair, brown eyes. When he died, this bounty man Charlie Wallace who I'd saved earlier in a big knife fight, knew that I was wanted. Charlie took me aside. He said, we could take Steerman's body to Fort Smith and collect the reward for Joseph Wainwright. That would do two things, free me and also we'd have some cash.

"It worked slick. We gave the federal clerk some of my things for proof. He never even looked at Steerman's body. He sent us to a funeral home without even peeking at him, and gave us a writ for the one hundred dollar reward."

She shook her head. "That's where you got the funeral idea, huh?"

"Well, it worked."

"So far." Her tone was skeptical.

"Well, you heard mine. How did you get in your line of work?" He pounded on the side of the horseshoe to narrow it for the dun's foot.

"When I was fourteen, a man and woman, in a nice surrey, came to our farm, dressed up like town folks and talking very educated.

They told my folks they needed girls to work in the homes of rich folks. They offered to pay a twenty-dollar bonus in advance against the first two months' pay. Oh, Mister and Missus Carley were real talkers. Convinced my folks I'd meet a rich man being a maid in one of those fancy Saint Louis houses.

"Room and board, thirty cents per day and nice uniforms to wear. Oh, it was a wonderful opportunity. That twenty bucks dangling out there for my poor folks. My paw agreed on account of the money. My mother cried. Saturday, they came by for me. Shirley Yeager was the girl I knew who went with all of us. The other two were the Pudding Sisters. I called them that because they were fat and dumb.

"We went to Saint Louis all right. The house was fancy too. And we were maids, but not to rich folks at their home. We were working in a whorehouse. The first night that they sold our bodies, Shirley hung herself in the closet. Guess I never had the nerve.

"A guy named Lucky Clover Murphy convinced me he loved me and hauled me out here to Arizona. I figured we'd get married sooner or later. But I lost the baby on the trip."

There was a long silence. Vince busied himself cold-shaping the shoe to fit the horse's foot. "That's how you got to New Field?"

"No. First, this LC Murphy was a loser. He began losing me and my body in his gambling. So I had to sleep with some grubby old man each time LC's luck ran out. I decided I could earn my own way doing that without him."

"Did it work?" A mouthful of nails muffled his voice as he pointed to the rasp he needed from her. Her story rang more tragic than his own. He'd never realized people would treat a woman so shabby.

She handed him the rasp. "LC caught up with me once and beat the hell out of me for leaving him. But I lighted out the next chance and I haven't seen him in four months."

"You figured this guy Allison in New Field would protect you from Murphy?"

"Exactly."

Nails pounded in the hoof, he drew in a deep breath and exhaled. "In the morning, we're heading for the high country. They say there's a ranch for sale up there."

"How much will it cost?" she asked.

"Too much probably. But we can go look."

"Do you have the money to buy one?"

He looked up at her, almost finished with the other hoof. "A couple hundred dollars. Why, have you got thousands?"

"Maybe eight hundred."

Then he let go of the horse's hoof and straightened. He was looking hard at her. "You told me you never stole —"

"I didn't. Come with me." She stalked off to the tent. He followed her, wondering what she meant and where she had the money stashed. When he ducked to enter the tent, he watched her lay the corset on the bed.

"Give me your knife," she said.

He lifted his hunting knife from the scabbard, wondering what she intended to do.

With a quick thrust, she cut the threads holding the material together, and to his disbelief, currency began to fall out. Some of the bills were old and worn, others newer. He looked up into her eyes as she held his big knife in one hand and the silky corset in the other.

"I earned that," she said. "I'll put my savings in, but I want a place with a nice house. That money was saved one night at a time."

"I thought you wanted silk and servants?" The currency didn't look like a stolen stash but rather added and sewn in as time had passed as she described. May kept opening more stashes in the undergarment and spilling out more money.

A tear slipped from beneath her eyelash and trailed down her tanned check.

"I want to be with you." She dabbed at the wetness with her fingertip. "I thought I'd hate living out here, and I do. But I knew when I was in the Apache camp I wanted to be with you no matter where that was at."

"I couldn't pay you back all this money if you changed your mind after I buy that place."

"Stupid," she sobbed and then hugged him. "I'm yours."

Vince looked across the desert as she pressed herself hard against him. His arms locked her to him. She was committed and they just might have enough money. He could hardly believe his good fortune.

Next morning he awoke excited. But she practically beat him getting dressed in the desert's cool predawn. He took some liberty watching her pull the jeans on her long slender legs in the starlight. In a few days, they might have a place of their very own. Maybe even sleep in a bed like other married men and women.

"I'll fix the food while you saddle up," she said, sitting on the ground to put on her squaw boots. "How did you find out about this place?"

"Oh, down at Walkers's store, last fall a man told us about it."

"Think it might be sold by now?" she asked, sounding cautious.

"There'll be something else for sale."

"Why up there?" she asked.

"Better grass and water. Cooler too. I hope I've spent my last summer down here in hell." He hurried after the stock.

Horses saddled, he sat on the nail keg with his plate of corn mush. She shot him a questioning look like there was something else on her mind.

"Good food." He waited. Something was eating her up but she never kept much to herself for long.

"Vince, every damn man in my life has lied to me. Carley sold me into white slavery, Murphy did the same, and Allison wants to kill me. I'm just worried about a double cross."

"Do you really think I would do that to you?"

"No, I don't want to, but whores ain't worth much," she said with a wry shake of her head.

"I never called you that."

"You don't have to. I know how men think."

"May? Have I ever lied to you or did one thing disrespectful to you?"

She shook her head.

"That's settled. If the gawdamn house ain't any good, we won't buy it. Fair enough?"

"Yes." She looked relieved.

Vince nodded. That was resolved. He sure hoped the place was as nice as the drifter had explained it to him and Pick Walters. May and him both needed a new start.

Midday, they crossed the saddle in the hills and headed down for the Verde, a small green line of trees far below them.

"The Army is here." Vince pointed to the tracks. "We'll probably run on to them before we reach the river."

"Sure," she said quietly and licked her lips with the tip of her tongue.

His mention of the Army had set her on edge. By now, he could sense her moods coming on. Why did she seem so uptight? They had nothing to fear from the military. Probably just out on a routine patrol with their Papago scouts. He wished at times he could read her mind. In the end he shrugged the notion away. When she was ready she would tell him.

He pointed out the dismounted line of soldiers to her before they reached the flats.

A lieutenant rode out to meet them, accompanied by sergeant with a heavy mustache.

"Howdy," the officer said. "This is Sergeant Fiffer, and my name's Bill Ruston."

"Vince Wagner and my wife May."

"Oh. Excuse me, ma'am." Ruston removed his hat. "We don't get many women folks out here. Nice to meet you Missus Wagner."

"Good morning," she said very evenly.

"Wagner, I've some business with you," the lieutenant said.

"What is that?"

"You haven't been trading with this hostile Chato have you?"

"Why is that?" Vince asked.

"My Papago scouts say that Chato is riding a blaze face horse you recently captured."

"The Apaches stole him and some others from our corrals," Vince said. May nodded in agreement.

"It's like them." The officer seemed to agree with the explanation. "When we capture them, I'll have the Papagos bring your horses back to you."

"I'd appreciate that," Vince said and motioned to May that they were going on.

"Have a nice day, ma'am. We'll see you,

Wagner," the officer said as they left them and went on to the river.

Being friendly, he waved at the line of dismounted soldiers resting their horses. Several flagged their hats friendly-like at May. But it was all in good taste and respect that men showed another's wife. Relieved the military incident was over, he let her go first across the ford. He followed on the black, leading the pack animal. The dingy, rushing water was stirrup deep as they splashed across.

Past the line of trees she pushed the worn hat back to ride on her shoulders, captured by the rawhide string at her throat.

"It worked," she said smugly.

"What's that?" He turned back to see if they were going to have any more interrogation by the military.

"My disguise worked," she said. "That Lieutenant William Ruston was an old customer of mine. He didn't even recognize me."

"She's dead," Vince said.

"Aren't you even a twinge jealous?"

"Nope. I've got you. All he has is a memory of a dead woman."

He smiled to himself when she turned back forward.

NINE

The desert gave way to sweet smelling junipers and pinyons as they gained altitude. Camped in a vast valley of brown grass, he unpacked and hobbled the horses while she made coffee and supper.

"This is sure lonely country," she said, bent over to get the coffee pot. "Why, all we've seen are jackrabbits, a coyote or two, and a few deer."

"We'll be in the tall pines in another day's ride," he promised her.

"You aren't forgetting our deal?"

"No ma'am. We ain't buying a ranch that does not have a house to suit you."

She grinned smugly at him. The rich steaming coffee looked good to him as she served it.

"You're something else, Vince Wagner."

"What's that?"

"I never figured I'd ever find a man like you."

"Is that good or bad?"

"Good for me. But —"

"Whatever is on your mind, say it."

She dropped her head and shook it. "I really hope we can buy this place and it has a house." She began to cry.

He scooted over and put his arm over her shoulder. "We'll have us a ranch of our own before this summer is over."

As he sat holding her, Vince wondered about the Army and the Papagos. They must be very close to Chato. If the scouts had seen the chief riding the bald-face horse, they might even know the very canyon where they were hiding.

Hugging her, Vince buried his face in her hair. The renegade Apaches' days were numbered. They had no place to go. At least so far two outcasts of society were making their way. He closed his eyes, savoring her closeness.

The next day, the stalwart Ponderosa pines carried a pungent resin fragrance. Wind swept through the boughs in a hushed song as they rode beneath the trees. Vince stopped at a store made of fresh sawn lumber. He ducked his head to enter the dark interior where the new wood smell of pitch blended with dry good odors.

"Howdy," the big man behind the counter

greeted.

"Vince Wagner."

"Sam Moffit, owner, proprietor, and chief Injun."

"Sam, a man told me there was a ranch for sale up here. I believe he said the Andrews place?"

"Sure is. Just go six miles up the right fork. On the right just before you ford Pine Creek. You thinking about settling here?"

"My wife and I. We're looking for a place."

"It's a good place. Live water in the creek year round."

"Thanks for the information." Vince dug in his pocket. "I'll take a couple twists of that licorice."

"My treat. If you buy that place, you'll be a customer."

"Is there a house on it?"

"A well-built log cabin. Miz Andrews's first husband built it before he got killed."

"Thanks." Vince took the licorice in his fist. "If we can buy it, we won't forget you."

"Why, have the Missus drop in any time. My wife will be sorry she missed her. She's gone berry hunting today."

"I will." Elated with the knowledge about the home on the Andrews property, he rejoined May and the horses.

She grinned at the handful of licorice he

111

handed her. "What did you find out?"

"So far so good," he assured her as he mounted. They both waved at the storekeeper. "There's a nice home on the place."

The low log cabin greeted them when they rode up. There was craftsmanship in the joists and the windows. He could tell a real particular person had built it. Just then a thin woman in a faded calico dress came out onto the porch.

Before they were close enough for the woman to hear them, May said, "Yes," in approval

Vince spoke over the barking cur dog as he removed his hat. "Good afternoon, ma'am. Is your husband home?"

"He'll be out directly. Have your wife get down and come inside." She shaded her eyes with the side of her hand. "We don't get many womenfolk up here to talk to."

"May, the Missus would like you to join her," Vince said.

"Yes." She jumped off the horse and hurried to tie it.

"This is May," he introduced her.

"Ellie's mine," she said. "My husband Cal's coming."

"I'm here." A lanky man younger than Vince expected stood in the doorway adjusting his galluses. Vince suspected he had been asleep. After introductions, the women went into the house.

"They told us at the store this place was for sale."

"Yeah, kinda nosey folks up there at Moffits's. Well, I've considered selling it. See, my wife ain't healthy. I figure maybe the place is kinda special. We got year round water and the rim up there blocks the bad storms."

"Must be kinda hard to sell this place, all the work you've done."

"Her health is the only reason. You haven't got a chew have you?"

"No, just the makings," Vince said.

"That's all right." He refused the offer. "I've got to go check on those lazy boys of hers. You know work builds character. I'm trying to instill that in her sons. See, her husband died a year ago, and I've been pressed to make those two boys understand about life since we got married. Course she's older than I am, but that don't matter does it?"

"I guess not," Vince said, growing weary of the man's words.

They walked to the big shed barn, the loft stuffed with loose hay. A milk cow's calf bawled as Cal pointed out the features and spoke of the extra cost items, like the fodder.

"Jefro! Buffer! Where are you boys?" he shouted.

"Coming, Mister Cal."

A youth of perhaps twelve came running out of breath, trailed by a younger brother.

"What have you boys been doing?" Cal demanded.

"Fixing the rail fence, honest. A deer must have gotten hung in it."

"You boys need to get in that corn patch," he reminded them sharply. "There better not be a weed in there, either or I'll bust your asses wide open."

"Yes sir," the oldest one said dutifully, and they rushed off to do the man's bidding.

"Idle hands make for idle minds. Ellie don't understand those boys of hers are lazy. I'm making men out of them. See, the reason I married her was I felt sorry for her. The poor woman needed a man to help her raise those boys. Me marrying her was the Christian thing for me to do. I could have had a much younger woman. Why, three or four neighbor girls fainted in disappointment when they heard about me taking on this big obligation."

"Cal, do you want to sell this place?" Vince asked, tired of the man's bragging.

He looked down the grassy bottom and listened to the milk cow's bawl.

"I'm asking one thousand dollars for it. That don't include the garden, hay, or the twenty-six stock cows, their calves, and two bulls."

Vince whistled through his teeth. "A mustanger like me would never make that kinda money in a lifetime."

"What's your offer then?"

"I could pay five hundred cash for all of it."

"That's robbery. Why I've turned down higher offers than that." Then in a low voice, "Do you have the cash money with you?"

"I probably could find it," Vince said, anxious to have his business concluded with this man.

Cal headed for the house. Vince wondered what he planned to do next. Had he accepted his offer?

"Woman! Pack your things that we can get in a wagon. I've sold this place," Cal announced.

The wilted look on Cal's wife's face did not escape Vince. May jumped up and said she was going to put their horses up.

Outside on the porch, Cal spoke again to Vince. "A well trained woman you got there." The man indicated May as she led the horses away. "She ain't bad looking either. Must have good raising, huh?"

Vince nodded. He couldn't forget how dejected Ellie looked at the news of the sale or how she shuffled out of the room like a very oppressed woman.

"My wife and I haven't had a real bed since we were married," Vince explained as if that was a long time. "You wouldn't have one for sale?"

"A great feather bed. Only cost you ten dollars. You want it?" Cal held out his palm for the money.

Vince paid him, anxious to escape the buffoon.

"Sold." Cal stuffed the money in his pants pocket before he shouted over his shoulder. "Ellie! Don't pack the goose down bed, I sold it too."

Vince excused himself. He wanted to confide with May.

At the barn, he found her gazing out at the meadow lined with the creek.

"Are you happy with this place?" he asked her. "There are twenty-six stock cows. With the dozen I have down on the desert, we'll have a good starting herd."

"Oh, Vince, I love this place. It's the poor woman worries me. That man will spend hers and the boys' remaining money." She sounded disappointed.

"If not us then someone else. I can't help it."

"Yes, I know Vince. I like the house. I'm just so upset about him." He hugged her. Tonight they would have their own bed. He could hardly wait. He shut his eyes as he listened to Cal impatiently calling in the boys.

The signed deed on the table, Cal had taken the wagon, Ellie, and the boys and left for the store to get an early start for Flagstaff in the morning. Vince shook his head. Ellie would never be well anywhere with him.

He looked across the table. "I want to have children with you."

She nodded, her eyes dancing in tears of pleasure and happiness. "We can try. I can't promise you. I have. . . ."

He rose, swept her up, and carried her to the bedroom. He kicked open the door.

"We have plenty of time," he assured her. Eager to be physically united with her, he did not want to waste the moments on words. They had years to talk of such things.

He placed her in the middle of the feather bed that was like a great pile of summer clouds. In a moment he undressed and joined her. Her tears tasted salty as they hungrily sought each other.

Somewhere on the rim above them, thunder rolled and grumbled. Vince heard it and wondered if it was a good or bad omen. Who did the thunder gods peal for? But he soon lost himself in May's exciting flesh and the pleasures she brought him.

Ten

The brockle-faced cow splashed her way out of the creek. Her new calf, with his tail flagged over his back, raced to keep up. There was no doubt in Vince's mind the cow was his. Her hide bore Cal's 77 brand. Vince reined up the black horse to let the pair settle down. No need for him to spook the cow-calf out of the country. He'd seen most of his newly acquired cattle in the past few days. The abundant mountain grama grass was strong feed and all the stock looked healthy.

Something moved in the pines on the slope. From the corner of his eye he caught sight of the figure. Cursing himself, he silently vowed never again to forget to buckle on the sidearm. He eased his hand for his saddle bag and the .44, chastising himself for being so busy counting his cows he'd forgotten there were any number of threats. Who was up there? If he had a rifle,

Vince was fair game. He could barely make out the outline of a horseman in the timber. The .44 in his hand, he wondered why they didn't shoot or speak out to him.

Dressed in a Sonora sombrero, the rider seemed hesitant to ride out in the open.

"Amigo!" the intruder finally shouted and waved as he hesitantly pushed his horse from the timber into the meadow.

Vince blinked to be certain. The *vaquero*-dressed rider was Juan Lopez. What was the Apache doing in the high country? Had he followed them? Vince warily searched the area. Nothing.

"I was not certain that you were alone, Vince," the man said, reining in his horse.

Vince looked him over. He hardly looked like the Apache warrior with whom he had negotiated May's return from his tribesmen. "What brings you to the mountains dressed like your father's countrymen?"

"Chato — everyone is dead." The grimness of Juan's words matched his stony face.

"How?" Vince could hardly believe every Apache in the band besides Juan had been killed.

"Our food was low. There was not much game. Chato sent me across the Rio Salado for some green corn the squaws had planted earlier. The moon of the green ears was

120

upon us. Then he took the people and slipped in our secret cave until the Army and the Papagos again left the mountains. But they found the cave and killed everyone."

"Women and children too?" Vince could hardly believe the Army capable of that kind of slaughter. The Papagos and Apaches were century-old enemies. They stole each other's children and women for slaves and wives. But for the Army to be involved in such an act shocked Vince. Folks certainly hated and feared the Apache.

Juan nodded. "My wife, my son, they died there with all the others. No one lived from all the bullets they fired into the cave."

The two men dismounted. Anxious to comfort him but feeling awkward, Vince put his hand on the man's shoulder. "I'm sorry, Juan."

"What will I do, Vince?" Juan asked.

"Become a *vaquero* and work for me," Vince said to lighten the man's mood. "I cannot bring back your dead relatives but you can stay with May and I."

"I could do this?"

"Damn right." Vince looked him over. "Those clothes ain't got any bullet holes in them do they?"

"No," Juan assured him. "They came from

a trunk I found."

"Good, white people are suspicious of bullet holes in clothing. Tonight, we'll cut your hair and you'll be a perfect Mexican ranch hand."

His dark eyes showed his relief. "Good, I came here because I thought you would help me. But I have some bad news for you."

Vince paused. What did he mean?

"I went by your camp to find your trail. While I was there two men in round hats rode into your camp and searched around. I wondered what they wanted and trailed them. They dug up her grave. They moved every stone, I watched them."

"Did you hear what they said?"

" 'She's not here.' " Juan looked questioningly at Vince.

The knowledge Allison's men had come back to validate her death only complicated his life more. Vince drew a deep breath. He should've killed them. In time they would find this place. He raised his eyes to study the towering wall of the Mogollon Rim. No place would be safe. Vince closed his eyes. He had failed her after all.

"What should we do?" Juan asked.

"Don't mention it to her, I must be the one to tell her myself. She will be very upset." Not only would May be shaken by the new knowledge, his own stomach churned as he considered the options for her safety. There had to be something he could do to stop Allison's killers from ever bothering her again.

Remounting their horses, Juan spoke, "The time is now gone but I wish you could have hunted the mountain sheep with Chato." The man shook his head. "He thought you were a strong man."

Vince nodded he had heard. Those hired gunmen were on his mind and what he must tell May. The pair rode in silence down the long meadow to the barn.

In her new blue dress, flush faced, May came running to meet them. Excitement was written in her expression as she held up the hem of the well-made garment to give herself the liberty of long strides. There were times in Vince's eyes when she expressed the innocent actions of a girl. His newfound knowledge niggled him even more.

"We have new chickens — Juan?" she gasped in disbelief. Her questioning look went to Vince. "What's wrong?"

"Juan has lost all his people. His wife, child, everyone was killed in a massacre. He has no one left alive and wants to be with us." Vince looked squarely at her for her approval.

"Why, yes of course, but what can we do?"

"There's nothing we can do." He drew a deep breath and squared his shoulders. "Did your hen's brood hatch?"

"Yes," she said, taken back by the news as the men unsaddled. "I was so excited I almost forgot. Juan, I'm so sorry for you."

The man indicated he understood.

"Another misfit," she said softly to Vince.

He agreed somberly and stripped the saddle off his horse.

Vince hated to fracture her happiness with what else he knew.

"Do you like my dress? I finished it today for a surprise."

"Yes, May, it's a very pretty dress. A good dress for my wife." She beamed and hugged him then she buried her face in his vest. "Two women came by today and asked us to come to the schoolhouse dance this Saturday night."

"What did you tell them?"

"That I would ask you," she said, like the world hinged on his answer.

"If you want to go, we'll go." He took her hand and headed for the house.

"You'll be proud of me," she promised.

"May, I'm always proud of you."

"Come on Juan," she said, looking back to be sure he was coming with them. "I have

124

some food cooked for you two."

Vince still didn't know how to tell her about Allison's rannies checking her grave. Half nauseated, he considered his options. He paused on the porch to wash his hands in the pan she'd set out. Life without her would be a great void. As he lathered his hands, he realized he never thought a woman could come to mean so much to him. Was there no justice? What could he do to stop Allison from chasing her over the face of the earth? Kill all of them? Maybe. He scowled as he dried his hands.

"Will I harm your new life here?" Juan asked, breaking Vince's concentration.

"No, Juan. It's her safety and those killers that I'm more worried about," he said under his breath. "I'm glad you came. You can be the eyes in the back of my head."

"You sure are taking your time," she said loudly, dishing food out on their plates and leaning over to watch for them.

"We're coming," Vince said, entering the room.

"I hope so, I've fresh vegetables from the garden —" She looked hard at Vince. "There's something else wrong isn't there?"

"I want you. . . ." He dropped his head. There was no way he could tell her to leave. At a loss for the words, he swallowed hard

125

over the knot in his throat. "Before he came up here, Juan saw Allison's men turn your grave upside down."

"Oh no!" She paled and slumped onto a high back wooden chair. "I thought it was all over. Vince, what will we do?"

"I'll sell some of the livestock to repay you. I can take you to the stage line and you can go to Denver, some place far away." He couldn't even look at her when he spoke. The whole notion knifed him.

"Then I'll take my chances here. With you. Where I belong. You don't want me to leave do you?" Tears filled her eyes. "Tell me for God's sake, Vince Wagner, that I belong with you."

He was without words and rushed to crush her to him. No, he was not going to let her leave, no matter what. He buried his face in her clean smelling hair. "I just want you to be safe."

"And the baby?"

"Baby?" He blinked his eyes in disbelief. "You have a baby?"

"Inside," she said, about to laugh. "Men and women do that."

"I know." It was hard to speak around the restriction in his throat. "When will it come?"

"Next spring." She tossed her head.

"We've completely forgotten our company. Juan, don't mind us. White men and women are different than Indians. We argue in public."

The fact they weren't alone as usual became instantly awkward, and they both gave a halfhearted laugh to make their guest feel welcome. Juan nodded that he understood and accepted it. The men sat at the table while she flitted about filling their coffee cups. Vince had a million questions on his mind to ask her about the baby. Had she ever given birth before? Did she have living children?

The Apache cleared his throat and both of them looked in his direction. "I feared you would hate me for those boys taking you prisoner." He gestured toward May.

She shook her head. "No. Those days with your people made me see how important Vince was to me."

"And you," he turned to Vince, "must hate me for costing you the horses to get her back."

Vince dismissed it with a shake of his head. "All that's over. You can work here as a ranch hand. The good Lord knows we can't pay much, but you're welcome to stay."

"Gracias, patrón," Juan said with a satisfied

smile. He began to eat with gusto.

Vince studied him for a moment. He did not intend to lose his family like Juan. Those killers were not going to ruin his life.

"From now on anywhere we go, you go," Vince said, pointing his fork at her.

May turned with the coffee pot in her hand. *"Sí, patrón."*

The three of them exchanged amused looks.

"And Juan, Mexicans drink coffee," May said, setting down her cup. "You better learn how," She poured his enamel cup half full.

He nodded. Vince couldn't tell whether he was pleased or displeased by her new direction. There were more pressing things to concern him. Juan would fit in just fine.

Smoke swept from the fire with the three long-handled branding irons sticking out like wagon spokes. May stood back of the smoldering pit. Her feet set apart, dressed in a newly made divided canvas skirt and outfit she'd sewn, she stood ready to bring an iron on their call.

The calf's hind legs ensnared by his lariat and towed behind his horse, Vince brought the doggie back from the bunch. He smiled at her as he dismounted.

Swiftly Juan moved in and flanked the calf

to the ground. While he suppressed the critter, May hurried forth with the red hot iron.

"Thanks." Vince took the long-handled steel implement and permanently marked the calf on his left hip in an acrid puff of smoke. Without looking, he handed her back the iron to reheat, and then knelt with his jackknife open to deftly remove the bull's seeds.

"You look hot," Vince said, looking into the sweat-glistened face of his cowboy.

"This sombrero is very hot." Juan shook his head.

"Ain't no fun dressing up is it?" Vince laughed at the man's discomfort and tossed the calf fries into the branding fire.

Juan straightened, releasing the calf to join his mother, who bawled in protest near the herd. Gingerly at first, the calf quickly recovered from his ordeal and headed for maw to find himself a handle to suckle milk from.

The pop of the splitting calf fry made both men whirl around in search of the treasure. Vince spied it and speared the seed on his jackknife. With a casual brush to remove a few particles of debris, he savored the sweet meat. Juan found the other and joined him.

"Oh, that's sickening," May said and

headed for the water bag hanging in the pine tree.

"Mountain oysters," Vince laughed. "Best food there is."

"Yuck." She shook her head. "You two are grisly today."

A big man on a stout buckskin mountain horse emerged from the timber. Vince stopped and his concerned look went to May who was the closest to the stranger. Who was this intruder?

"Howdy folks," the man said with a big smile. "Didn't mean to startle you none. I'm Cy Perkins from the Box Cross just over the way. You must be the Wagners?" He looked at the three of them. "My missus came over yesterday."

"Oh, yes," May said. "Vince, she and the other lady invited us to the dance."

Vince nodded a greeting. He certainly must not be one of Allison's men. The damn Colt . . . if he didn't go to wearing it all the time, he would have no one to blame if they rode in and took her away because he wasn't armed to stop them.

"See you're branding," Perkins said.

"Our own cattle," Vince said carefully.

"I know that. I tell you, that no good Andrews wasn't worth the powder to blow him up." Perkins dismounted heavily and sighed.

"Everyone around here was concerned when she took up with him. Hope her and those boys make it, wherever they went."

"Flagstaff. That's where he said they'd go when he left." May offered him the water bag as a sign of neighborliness.

"I'm Vince Wagner, this is my *vaquero* Juan Lopez." The men held a round of hand shaking.

"Moffit never mentioned a ranch hand," Cy said, shaking each man's hand.

"Juan just came up from our other place down in the basin," Vince explained. Was the Apache's presence going to be a problem? He scolded himself for making more of the matter than existed. No, he was just a Mexican ranch hand.

"If you can spare him, I could use the help. I've got some late ones needs an iron put on their butts — excuse me, ma'am."

May just shook her head wistfully, tickled at the big man's politeness. Vince tried to suppress his amusement. Anyway, her role as his wife had Perkins convinced. She'd certainly heard worse than "iron on his butt" in her past.

"We can spare him to help you a day or two," Vince offered.

"Be fine. Can't afford me a full-time hand."

"Juan's been part of our family. Guess he likes May's grub line," Vince said. "Sure ain't the pay."

Juan nodded and grinned. Vince felt satisfied their disguises had worked with the man.

"Reason I came, there's been some horse rustling. I saw the smoke and wondered if it was them," Cy said. "I'm looking for a bay and a buckskin, saddle stock I turned out. They usually stay over east. If rustlers didn't get 'em, the damn Apaches may have."

"Have you seen any Indians?" Vince asked.

"Hell, who sees damn Apaches? Couple days ago, they stole a damn ham off my back porch, never woke the dogs doing it either. They could steal horses a damn sight easier than that."

"We sure haven't seen any Indian sign," Vince said.

"Keep your eyes peeled. They may come through here." Perkins prepared to remount. "You're coming to the dance, ain't you?"

"The missus said we should. Guess we'll see you then."

Perkins nodded and swung his horse around to leave. He waved goodbye, then rode off into the pinyons. Vince watched Perkins's horse cat-hop with effort up the slope under the big man's weight. He soon disappeared in the timber.

"Was the ham salty?" he asked Juan when Perkins went out of sight.

A slow smile spread across his dark face. "Not very good."

"I think he bought us," May said. "I don't have a doubt that he thinks I'm your wife and Juan is our cowboy."

"I know he did. But we were careless. He could've been one of Allison's men and all of us could have been dead."

"But Vince, we can't spend all our time living in fear," she protested.

He didn't answer. "Juan, put out the fire and you take May home. I'm riding to Moffits's store. If they're in the area, they'll likely stop there first. I need to check and see if they're around."

"Vince." She trailed after him to the horse. "Whatever you do be careful."

He drew a deep breath and kissed her on the cheek to reassure her that he would. "You and Juan do the same." He reached past her and jerked the repeater out of his scabbard. "You may need this, Juan."

"Must you go looking for trouble?" she asked.

"If they're here, I want to know. I'll be home by midnight. Go on with Juan."

She shook her head with a look of dread,

but obeyed.

Mounted, he removed the Colt and gun belt from his saddlebag and strapped it on. He hated to disappoint her, but Vince needed to know if the hired guns were in the mountains. He loped the black horse westward toward Moffits's Store.

ELEVEN

There were a few rigs parked outside the raw wood-framed store. The last rays of sundown lanced through the tall ponderosa pines that sheltered the store and small warehouse. Cautiously, Vince circled around, checking the two hitched saddle horses in back that bore F T brands and obviously belonged to some outfit close by.

He dismounted and tied the black beside the pair. There was no sign of their riders. Careful to survey the area, he headed for the front porch.

Two youthful cowboys sat on the stoop with their jackknives spearing peach halves from open tin cans. With sticky juice dripping down their chins, they made an attempt to wipe it off.

Vince nearly laughed aloud as his worst suspicions melted. He could remember when a can of fruit was better than any bottle of whiskey and a lot longer-remembered treat.

"Sure looks like powerful fun," he said to them and pushed his way in the store.

Their good-natured reply was lost as he entered the world of harness oil and dry goods' strong odors. He touched his hat for two women folk who looked up at him when he moved toward the counter and the big man in the canvas apron, Sam Moffit.

"How's ranching?" Sam asked with a wide grin.

"Good, we've been busy. Say, there hasn't been anyone asking for me has there?"

"No." Sam shook his head. "You expecting company?"

Vince lowered his voice. "Not the kind I'd be proud of. A pair of gunfighters in bowler hats. It's an old story. But don't intervene, Sam. They're hard cases."

"I don't need to know anything," the storekeeper said, slowly nodding his acceptance. "But I'll send the oldest boy first thing to warn you if they come here."

"I'd appreciate that," Vince said, checking on the two shoppers who seemed disinterested in their conversation. He didn't need to everyone knowing his business or his problems.

"You and the missus are coming to the dance Saturday night ain't you?" Sam asked in an normal tone of voice.

"Guess so. My wife's looking forward to it." Vince said loud enough to draw nods of approval from the two women. "Give me five cents' worth of licorice and the same in hard candy. My Mexican ranch hand came up this week."

"Bet you're getting lots done up there," Sam commented as he filled the order.

Vince left the coins on the counter and took the poke. "We're getting lots done, and she said to tell you that last material was fine."

"See ya Saturday night," Sam called after him.

He paused on the porch and drew in a deep breath of the pine resin smell in the air. There was a new scent on the breeze. Then he heard the distant grumble of thunder. He nodded to the two peach eaters opening their second can apiece, and headed for his black horse. He could use some moisture on the crops and the range grass. The tow sack of candy in his left hand, he remounted. The killers weren't there yet.

Yellow light from the reflector lamp shone from out the narrow windows as he approached the house. Plentiful thunder rumbled on the rim to the north, with

137

flashes of lightning illuminating the treetops as the storm gathered. A fresh damp breeze swept his face as he dismounted. May had waited up for him.

"That you Vince?" she called from the house.

"Yes, I'll be there. It's about to rain." He started as a gust of hard wind loosened his hat and he was forced to stay it. He dumped the saddle on the porch and unbridled the black to turn him loose in the yard.

The deluge began to rap on the roof as he entered the house with the precious cargo in his fist. "Raining good now —"

He paused. Juan stood in the middle of the main room with dress material draped on him. "Well, May has a new sewing helper I see. Here, have some candy for your pay."

Juan accepted it and shook his head. "White men must do strange things." Both men nodded in agreement.

May looked up at them with a scowl. "How else will I ever get my clothes made? I durn sure couldn't pin them on myself."

Vince put a piece of hard candy in her receptive open mouth. "Anything Juan will stand for is fine."

She rose and took the material off Juan and folded it. When she turned the serious-ness returned to her face. "No sign of them

138

at the store?"

"None. Sam Moffit is going to send us word if they show up at his place."

"The candy's good. I forgive you for leaving me." Behind her effort to suck on the rock piece, she smiled teasingly.

There was a blinding streak of lightning and thunder shook the whole cabin. May bolted upright as if shot and slapped both hands on the table. "I hate storms."

"Thunder gods," Juan said from the doorway where he viewed the weather. "They talked to the Apaches."

"What did they say?" she asked.

"I don't think I can speak to a white woman about such things," Juan said as if taken aback by her question.

"I'm sorry," May said with a shake of her head. "I didn't mean to remind you of your losses."

"That is all right. The thunder gods spoke to the medicine man."

The next bolt and crash, Vince caught her in his arms as if to help protect her.

"They once told him the Apaches would always own the land like the white man does now."

He moved in to help protect her. She was like a whirlwind and pushed free of his grasp in panic.

"What the hell are they saying now?" she screamed hysterically.

"They're saying that it's raining," Vince said in her ear to calm her. "I won't let anything happen to you and the baby."

She clung to him. "I know, Vince. I just hate storms." She trembled inside. And then shivered in his hug with the next blast.

"It is a corn rain," Juan said to him. "The corn will grow full in the husk with this rain. It is a good sign for us." He started to leave them. "I will look around."

"Be careful, *amigo.* Come get me if you find them," he said with his arms around her and holding her against his chest.

"I will." Juan took his sombrero from the nail and went out the back door.

Vince listened to the steady rain. If anyone could find them before they crept up on the ranch, Juan could. Vince blew out the lamp and she led him by the hand to their featherbed.

With the dawn, diamonds of rain drops glistened on the pine boughs. Arms over his head, stretching his back, Vince stood in the doorway and surveyed his washed kingdom. Behind him, May rattled the cast iron lids to her cook stove and built a fire for breakfast.

"Juan never came back last night," she said.

Vince turned and nodded he knew. "He'll be all right."

"Another thing, Vince Wagner. I want you to put that black horse outside of my yard. I fully intend to have flowers, maybe roses, and I don't appreciate that black gelding's head stuck in my door either."

He grinned after her as she went to draw water for the coffee pot. When she re-appeared, he smiled in surrender. "Won't happen again."

"I doubt that." She set the pot down. "What are we doing today?"

"Moving the black horse," he said peeking at May for her reaction while he rolled a cigarette.

"What else?"

"Check the rail fence around the corn. Mule deer can eat you out of house and home. So can a black bear if he ever gets a taste for it."

"Do you think Juan found something?" she asked.

"He's a big boy, May. He'll be fine."

"Who's grouchy now?"

Vince shook his head to dismiss her comment and puffed on the cigarette. Wherever Juan was, Vince couldn't run off to help him. Besides, having been an Apache, Juan could survive where a white man would be exposed. Slowly Vince exhaled. He had to wonder where the Apache was all night.

The corn looked recovered despite the drought-streaked leaves that were rustling in the cool air. As they circled the field on their inspection tour, Vince never saw a single wild animal track nor rail disturbed around the patch. May trailed along picking wild daisies and making a chain with them.

"The corn will be good," he said, standing on the second rail to survey more of it.

"You sound like my father. What big ears. Going to fatten all our hogs —"

"Hush!" he said. "Do you hear horses coming?"

"It's the Army," she said as the yellow guidon came in view down the meadow.

Vince could see them coming. The troopers in columns of two, and the Papago scouts stringing along. There were three other Indians with them on horseback in chains.

"Oh God, Vince, they've got prisoners."

"Control yourself," he said under his breath. Half sick with the notion Juan might be among the arrested ones, he tried to see the faces of the renegades.

When she turned back, May pulled down

the floppy brim of her hat. But not before Vince saw the scowl on her face.

Lieutenant Ruston held up his yellow-gloved hand and the noncom ordered, "Halt."

"Mister Wagner, we meet again," the officer said, touching his hat. "And good day, Missus Wagner."

"Thanks. What brings the cavalry up here, Ruston?" Vince looked over the dust-floured soldiers. He could see two of the prisoners and did not know them. Was Juan the third one? Hatless, it was hard for him to tell, since they were farther back in the column.

"We had a battle with Chato and the hostiles in the Brakes. Got most of them. Oh, we killed thirty bucks, I imagine. We've captured these three renegades but one more got away. Papagos think he headed up here."

Vince shook his head. "I can't tell you. Never seen any since we came." May shook her head beneath the hat. For a moment, Vince glimpsed the third prisoner's long hair and to his relief, knew it couldn't be Juan. The hair was too long.

One of the Papago scouts rode forward on the bald-face horse.

"They never eat this one." He patted the horse's neck like he treasured it.

143

Vince knew the scout just wanted to taunt him. Possession was nine-tenths ownership when an animal wasn't branded. But the fact the lieutenant had said they'd killed thirty bucks galled Vince worse than the horse. They'd counted Juan's wife and child as one if they did. Chato never had that many soldiers in the best of times.

"We haven't cut any sign, but I figure these Papagos led us to Chato's cave, they can find one stray one," the officer said.

"I'll keep an eye out," Vince said.

"This buck could be desperate. If he realizes he's the last living tribesman he might go on a killing rampage." Ruston reined his horse around as if ready to move out. "Oh, I sure hope I didn't upset you ma'am. Just can't be too careful about these hostiles."

"I understand lieutenant," she said coldly.

The guidon disappeared up the meadow.

Their file gone from view, she spoke first. "Why did Ruston seem so intent on saying things to me?"

"No reason." Vince shook his head in disapproval. "The son of a bitch considers himself a lady's man. Wanted to impress the hell out of you. Besides, he didn't want to miss a chance to flirt with my wife."

"That's all?"

"That's all," he assured her.

144

"You don't like him?" she asked as they headed for the house.

"I call him the butcher of Rio Salado." He shook his head to free himself of the grim vision of the slaughter. "He's a snob, May. Riding down the meadow like he owned this place. Some sort of high and mighty lord. And he let that damn Papago scout flaunt that bald-face horse at me. I bet he put that Indian up to it. What did he say at the Verde, that he'd return my stock?" Vince drew a deep breath through his nose. He hoped Ruston's horse fell down and rolled over on the brass-buttoned pompous ass.

"Last night, did his thunder gods warn Juan?" she asked softly.

Vince took a sweeping look around the valley. "Maybe they did May. They just might have."

"He's all right," she said as they resumed walking. "I know he is." She pushed the hat back on her shoulders and smiled at Vince.

He agreed. But where were Allison's killers? They were somewhere.

TWELVE

The clear call of the rooster quail came on the wings of darkness. Awakened by the whistle, Vince strained to hear. No mistaking the sharp two-note song of the game bird. On his elbows, he listened to May's soft breathing beside him. She was sound asleep. Was Juan outside signaling to him? Apaches used the bird call to locate each other during a hunt or attack to tell the others where they were.

Quietly, he slipped off the bed so as not to disturb her and pulled on his jeans. His fingers closed on the smooth wooden handle of the .44. Vince cocked his head to listen. The call came again.

Satisfied Juan was signaling him, he slipped through the dark house illuminated only by the dim starlight that frosted areas beneath the windows.

On the porch Vince scented the piney air, fresh with the night coolness. He watched

Juan slip from the dark shadows of the trees and cross the yard.

"You all right, *amigo*?" Vince asked. "I guess you know the damn Army was through here looking for you. They had three Apaches in chains."

"The pony boys and army look for the wind," Juan said as the two men sat on the porch's edge.

"Would those prisoners tell the Army about you?"

"No, they saw me. I wanted to free them but they shook their head."

"Shook their head?" Vince could not understand their refusal of his aid.

"Too risky. Besides, the Army will free them in San Carlos after the Papagos insult them all the days going back."

"So the rumors of the wild renegade Apache on the loose will persist?" Vince asked, amused by the insight. "Any sign of the gunmen?"

"No, but I've found the camp of those who steal the horses."

"You know where the horse thieves are?"

"Yes, I'm sure. I've heard them talk how easy it is to take the stock."

Vince wished for his cigarette makings. Saliva flooded his mouth. "I sure thought Allison's gunmen would be up here by now."

147

Juan shook his head.

Vince stood up and stretched, still perplexed by the delay of the killers and wondering what he must do about the horse rustlers. Tell Perkins in the morning. "There are beans on the stove. Get something to eat. I think your disguise as a *vaquero* will work."

"*Sí, patrón,*" Juan said and went inside.

Vince headed back for the side room. Entering, he saw May sitting up in her white night shirt, so he closed the board door for their privacy.

"What's wrong?" Her voice was thick with sleep as she swept her short hair up.

"Nothing, Juan's back. And there's no sign of the killers." He sat on the edge of the bed, restoring the Colt to the holster.

"You got up in the middle of the night for that?" she asked in disbelief.

Vince shed his britches and crawled into the bed. There were times he wished she wouldn't be so damn obstinate. He kissed her and eased her down beneath him. His mouth silenced her. He'd explain it all later — for now he had other notions. He raised himself to push up her cotton shift to expose her smooth skin. What would he do without her. . . .

Sun streamed in the side window. The

gentle wind waved her kitchen curtains. May's back was to him as she turned the hot cakes on the stove.

"Did you tell Juan about the bald-face horse?" she asked.

"He saw him."

"What are you going to do about the horse thieves Juan found?" she asked.

"I'm headed for Perkins after breakfast to see what he wants to do. They're his horses."

She turned, about to say something, then shook her head. "Guess it's all you can do."

"It could be our stock."

"Oh, I know."

"What's eating you?" he asked, unaccustomed to her not speaking her piece.

"I just don't want anything to happen to you."

"Thanks, I'll take special care." He turned as Juan entered the kitchen from the back porch. "Morning."

"Bet you missed my coffee," she said with a wide smile.

Juan nodded. "I did miss it." He nodded to them and took a cup for her to fill. "I like being a *vaquero* better than to sleep on the ground."

They laughed.

After breakfast, Vince set out for Perkins's. The rustling maturing corn he passed

149

reminded him that fall would soon be bringing cooler weather. At this altitude, the season would be much colder than at his desert outfit.

At the Perkins ranch, dogs heralded his arrival. A faded green wagon with a skeleton of ash bows sat before the log cabin. Perkins emerged, shouting at the black-and-tan hounds to be quiet.

"Good morning, Wagner. Come on, there's coffee left." Perkins curled his arm in a wave.

Seated at the oak table in the low-trussed house, Vince sipped on coffee. Perkins's wife, Selma, was a straight-backed woman with a warm smile, anxious to know how they liked the mountains, and did they plan to attend the dance. Vince assured her they would.

"Juan found the horse thieves' camp," Vince told Cy when they were alone.

"Damn. I hate horse thieves." Perkins shook his head warily. "I'll ride over and get Clay Emerson. He's a good man and will want to go with us."

"How long will that take?" Vince asked.

"We'll be in the south end of your meadow in a couple of hours with fresh horses and ready to ride. How far is it?"

"Juan knows, but it can't be over a half

days' ride."

"Selma," Perkins called out. "We'll be riding after those rustlers."

She came into the room and looked at her husband with a frown. "You two need to be careful. Andrews was killed by some saddle tramps stealing his horses."

"Selma, we will." Perkins strode over and took a well-oiled Winchester off the mantle.

"We should be back some time tonight," Vince said.

"Yes," she said with a nod. "Tell your missus I hope she'll come visit me. May was her name, wasn't it?"

"Yes, it's May. I will tell her," Vince said. "See you at the meadow. Juan'll be with me. He knows the way."

"Clay and I'll be there," Perkins promised as the two men parted.

Vince watched them come from the hillside behind the barn, Juan with a shovel, May carrying a plant. He dismounted the black and waited for them.

"I found a rose for the yard," she said, and without stopping, headed for the house. "A wild one."

"May, we're going after those rustlers. Juan and me." Vince smiled. "I wouldn't leave you alone at all but I better ride with

151

Juan and the others to see about these rustlers."

"I'll be fine," she said, obviously involved in planting the bush she bore.

"We need for them to believe he's a cowboy.

She agreed. "They do need to believe that. We'll plant this by the side of the porch."

"Do all *vaqueros* do such work?" Juan asked with a private look he shared with Vince as they rounded the house.

"Just the good ones." She pointed out where she wanted the hole dug.

Vince wondered about the thieves. He stood back and watched May pack dirt around the plant.

"You two go on. I'll be fine," she assured them. "I've got to water this rose."

He studied her as she worked to be sure everything was just so with the plant. When she realized he was still there, she used her forearm to shade the sun and looked up at him. "I'll be fine. Go on."

"Just checking."

"I'm doing good. I can remember being sick every day when I was pregnant before. I must be stronger now."

"I hope so, May." He nodded and hurried behind the house to join Juan, who held the reins to his horse. He certainly wanted everything to be all right for her.

In the end of the long meadow, Perkins rode up with the shorter man, Clay Emerson. They introduced each other and let Juan take the lead.

"How far is it to their camp?" Perkins asked from behind.

"In the junipers," Juan said.

They dropped out of the high country. The two ranchers appeared nervous. Vince caught them searching around warily several times.

"I never thought they'd ride off into this Apache land," Perkins said in a low voice. "This is right where those renegades of Chato stayed."

Emerson agreed, searching around suspiciously as he rode. "If the Army didn't have the Apaches out of here, I'd sure think they'd took the horses, where we're headed."

Juan turned in the saddle and grinned. "These horse stealers are *gringos.*"

Both ranchers laughed. Riding behind them, Vince heard their conversation and the amusement, but he also heard the strain in the men's laugh. Horse rustling was a serious matter, and the gravity of the situation ate at his stomach. There were matters ahead of them that needed to be dealt with in a stern fashion. Vince drew a deep breath and pushed his shoulders back. He didn't like to think about it, but he would.

After two more hours of riding, Juan pointed to a side canyon left in the towering sandstone bluffs. "Their camp is in there."

"Maybe they're gone," Perkins said with disgust.

"They're still there," Juan assured them.

Vince remained at the rear of the line, listening to the men's conversation. Niggled by the fact May was home alone, he tried to act interested in the capture of the outlaws.

The juniper and pinion surrounding them were taller than a rider when they pulled up. A tan, sedimentary, wind-eroded face of the mountain towered high over them. The slash was knife-like where the canyon opened. A lone buzzard circled lazily on the updraft.

"These rustlers are going to try and run for it when we jump them," Perkins said when they gathered for a confab. "What's this place like?"

"Just a shelter and a brush pen," Juan said.

"How many?" Clay asked.

"Two." Juan held up his fingers.

They decided to split up to close any possible escape routes. Vince agreed to go up on the slope to the left, Perkins the south,

154

and Clay with Juan took the middle. The men drew out their weapons and set spurs to their horses. The element of surprise must be their advantage.

Vince could see nothing but the brushy junipers as he urged the black horse forward. Two shots rang out. Emerging from the thicket, he saw a bare-headed cowboy blasting at Clay and Juan as they bore down on him. Vince reined up the black and snapped a shot at the rustler. The man went down. A second figure dressed in chaps crumpled over beyond the pen in a hail of Perkins's bullets. Almost before it began it was over. Both rustlers were on the ground and the four of them were unscathed.

Perkins dismounted and cautiously turned over the one beyond the corral. The rancher rose, shaking his head. The rustler was done for.

Clay knelt beside the other outlaw. Vince was taken aback by the rustler's pained face, the blood blooming on his shirt. My gawd, just a mere boy.

"They went to shooting," Clay said with a wry shake of his head.

"Mister —" The dying cowboy gasped. "Don't tell my ma. It would kill her."

Vince silently agreed as he recognized him. They were the same boys he'd spoken

155

to eating canned peaches at the store.

No, they'd never tell his ma.

"That one's name is Bonner," Perkins said as they all removed their hats in reverence. "The one over there was Skip something. Drifted in here last spring. Got laid off after roundup. Must have stayed up here stealing horses."

"They had two F T horses at the store the other night," Vince added. "Should we bury them here?"

"Just as well. Ain't no kin close I know of," Perkins said. "Them's mine and Ben's horses in the pen."

Vince looked around at the yellow tarp half-shelter and the meagerness of their camp. He'd known hardship and isolation in his years in the desert. Damn little in this place to die for. A half-dozen stolen horses worth maybe twenty bucks apiece. A couple of old dried out saddles, threadbare saddle blankets, and the two of them went to hell in some run down patched boots.

He glanced over at Juan, satisfied Perkins and Emerson were out of hearing range.

"This is stupid. Them dying for some hundred dollars' worth of gear and broom-tails." Vince shook his head in disapproval.

Juan nodded. "But sometimes it is better to die than live like a starving dog."

156

Perhaps. Vince wasn't certain. Juan knew of such things. But these boys needed whipped not killed. "We better go help them."

"Whiskey either of you?" Perkins offered. "Gawdamnit, Vince. I never shot no kids before." Pained looking, the rancher took a deep draught from the neck of the bottle and handed it to Emerson when both Vince and Juan declined the offer.

There were plenty of rocks to cover them so the varmints couldn't dig them up. Perkins and Emerson were nearly drunk by the time the grave was done. Vince considered the two ranchers lucky. He felt certain he was going to be sick before it was over. He heaved a great sigh of relief when the crude funeral was completed and he hadn't vomited.

THIRTEEN

Moonlight silver laced the meadow. In silence, he and Juan rode their jaded horses close to the creek's gurgle. Too weary to think straight, he looked forward to being home with May. The sight of the lighted windows in the cabin filled him with relief. She must be there and all right. His deepest concerns dissolved at the sight of her coming from the house.

"About time you two drug in," she said, greeting them from the doorway.

"We've been coming." He sighed and dismounted.

"You sound worn out." She took him in her arms and laid her head on his shoulder as they hugged each other.

"It's been a bad day, May." He shook his head. "The rustlers were just boys and they fought for it."

"Oh, God, I'm sorry."

Vince tried to clear his head. "Guess the

best thing we did today was convince Perkins and Emerson that Juan really was a *vaquero.*"

"That's good. Come on, I've got food," she offered as the men stripped off their saddles. "It may be overcooked."

"It'll be fine. We're starved. Turn 'em loose," he told Juan about their mounts. "Tired as these horses are, they won't go far."

"I found another wild rose bush today and moved it," she said to liven up the conversation on the way to the house.

"Good," Vince said, wondering how many more brambles she intended to bring in. "Anyone come around?"

"No."

"Good." He smiled for her sake.

In the middle of the meal, his strength recovered from the food and coffee, Vince began to think about the approaching fall.

"When it cools off, I want to get some venison to eat," he announced.

"Elk," Juan said, pointing his spoon in the direction of the rim.

"I never shot one," Vince admitted. "They're big. Are they good to eat?"

Juan nodded with a grin. "Plenty good eating."

"Will you be able to go with us?" he asked

May, concerned about her pregnancy.

"Certainly," she said. "Why Apache women step off horses and have babies and ride on. Don't they Juan?"

"Yes." He looked up and slowly nodded in agreement. "I could not tell you before, but today, I saw some tracks of two shod horses I had not seen before."

"You don't think they're in the country?" May asked him anxiously. Pausing as she refilled their coffee cups, she waited for an answer.

"We'll just have to be careful," Vince said. "The tracks might just be someone drifting through."

"But you really don't believe that do you?" May asked.

"How could I know?" Vince inhaled sharply. "We'll keep a keen eye out. Folks like Allison don't give up easy, we know that."

He looked at the two of them as they solemnly nodded in agreement. Somehow he would have to settle the matter with this man himself if there was ever to be an end to the wondering and speculation.

"Good night," Juan said, rising from his chair. "The food was good."

"Thanks, Juan," May said.

They sat in silence. Vince savored his coffee, letting a lot of the day's tension drain.

"It was a very bad day for you?" She reached for his free hand and squeezed it in hers.

"I'm glad it's over is all."

She forced a smile. "Let's go to bed."

Her notion sounded inviting in his present state of mind. He rose and blew out the lamp on the table.

Vince used some of their money to buy a team, harness, and wagon. The part Percheron team was only green broke and Juan had to snub one to his saddle horn to prevent a runaway while Vince drove them. Each day they worked them in the long, open meadow, wearing the big horses into submission.

"I'll try driving them back to the house without you holding them," Vince announced

"Plenty powerful horses." Juan looked like he doubted Vince's ability to hold them in check.

"They'll do fine," Vince said, the leather reins threaded through in his fingers. Tensed, he began the drive back. The horses' feathered legs pumped as they went.

"We need to bring the rest of my cattle up here and put the 77 brand on them," he said to Juan, who rode beside the wagon. The horses were eager-acting, but seemed to be all right.

"When?" Juan asked.

"Before she's too pregnant to go with us."

The *vaquero* nodded that he understood. Vince studied the rim high above them. He was lucky to have Juan helping him and her — especially May. Where were Allison's rannies hiding themselves? There had been no other sign.

She came out to meet them. "Can we drive the new team to the dance?"

"I guess the trip would do them good," Vince said, dismounting. "I've been thinking I may have forgotten how to dance."

"When you hear the music, it'll come back," she assured him. "Can we stay all night?"

"I reckon." He saw no reason not to. Something caught his attention and he turned to listen.

"Geese!" she shouted as the honk of the birds became more apparent.

Fall wouldn't be far behind the migratory birds. He shook his head. They still had lots of work to do before winter cold set in.

Vince swelled with pride as he reined the big horses into the grassy opening sur-

162

rounding the whitewashed one-room school house. May wore her new blue dress and shawl. She sat on the seat beside him. Her hair freshly Dutch bobbed, her good looks radiated when he glanced over at her.

"I may even smile," she whispered as he set the brake.

"Do that," he said.

"I want you to be proud of me," she said, with a note of concern in her voice.

"You just be yourself. I'll be proud enough."

"Howdy mister," a freckle-faced youth said, admiring the horses. "That's sure some team."

"Vince Wagner," he introduced himself as he stepped down.

"Tuffy Holms."

"Tuffy, are you good at driving horses?" He helped May down, and looked the kid in the eye.

"Yes, sir."

"Get up there," Vince said. "You can drive them easy-like around the yard. Don't let them run. You can make a round or two around the clearing here."

"Wow! Thanks." Cat-like, the youth sprung on the seat and carefully undid the lines. His attention centered on the team.

"Take your time," Vince cautioned him.

"I will."

The horses started very slow and seemed to be without life as they went. May frowned at Vince. "What's wrong?"

"The horses know the boy doesn't have the authority in his voice or in his hands that transfer commands to their mouths."

May smiled. "You've made him happy anyway."

"You go ahead." He motioned toward the schoolhouse.

"The Perkinses are here." Skirts in her hand she headed for the front door.

Perkins joined him and warned in a friendly tone, "That boy may leave with that team."

A group of men gathered around Vince. He shook hands with Jim Harvey of the H C and several others.

"We're the non-Mormons," Harvey announced. "The Mormons will be along. They never miss a dance. Kinda clannish and don't approve of everything we do."

Harvey's words drew a laugh from the others.

"They don't believe in drinking," Perkins injected.

"Aww," Emerson scoffed. "Some do." His words drew more laughter.

Vince directed the boy to park the team,

then busied himself unharnessing with the excited youth assisting him.

"You and the missus like it up here?" the boy asked.

"Sure do," Vince said.

"You ever need a favor you just call on me." In a flash, the boy was gone with his impressed friends.

Vince finished putting a tie rope between two pines to hitch the horses for the evening. When he checked around, he decided May was inside with the womenfolk. He sauntered over to join the men.

"They say you've got another herd?" Harvey looked concerned.

Vince smiled. "It won't crowd the range. There's just a dozen more pair of cows and calves."

"We're getting a lot of cattle in this country," Harvey said.

He nodded. He understood the man's concern. The rancher seemed very worked up over the prospect of more stock on the range.

"Is it true that you break horses?" a new man asked in an effort to lighten the conversation. "Tom Shanks," the man belatedly introduced himself.

"Yes, I do," Vince said.

"I'll bring a half-dozen head for you to

break next week."

Vince nodded. He and Juan could earn some money. He wondered how May was doing with the womenfolk. Perhaps he should go inside in case she needed saving from a situation.

"What do you charge to break one?" another asked.

"Ten bucks if they ain't plumb outlaws." Vince grew more anxious. Was May all right? Had the women of the community accepted her?

"I've got a Jersey cow. You need a milk cow?" another rancher asked. "She's a good one and I'd sell her worth the money."

"I'd look at her." Vince knew the cow he'd bought with the place would soon be dry. "How much?"

"Oh, fifteen dollars sound fair?"

"I'll be by to look at her in the next week."

"Mormons are coming." Perkins jerked his thumb as a convoy of buckboards, wagons, and riders filed in.

Vince looked them over as reserved cordial greetings were exchanged between the two groups. He couldn't tell a lot of difference as he shook hands with the menfolk. Acknowledging the reservation between the two factions, he dismissed the matter.

Inside the schoolhouse, he found May

helping the womenfolk put desserts on the table. As the fiddles began to play, young and old were up to dance.

"How is it going?" he asked her.

"Very good. I've bought a mother cat and five chickens to go with my small flock, including a Shanghai rooster. My mother use to sell eggs for grocery money. By spring, I should have a real laying flock."

Vince shook his head. He'd been worried about her? She might have become more a part of them than he was. "I'm going to look at Jersey cow for you too. I want her fresh when the baby comes."

May agreed and they danced off into the crowd on the floor. He smiled to himself. He did remember how to dance. Pride swelled up inside his chest. May was one of the prettiest women there. He was damn sure lucky.

The fight broke out of nowhere. Two boys in their teens were tight-mouthed and swinging fists at each other in the parted crowd.

"She's my sister and she ain't going out with no damn Mormon like you!"

"Like to see you stop me!"

A rash of blows and neither seemed to have an advantage. The girl rushed off holding back a dam of tears. Obviously she was

167

more hurt than the sparring young men.

"You get him!" Cy Perkins shouted to Vince as he prepared to throw his arms around the other youth. "Enough. You boys should be ashamed, fighting at a dance like some barroom trash."

He caught her brother by the arm and guided him toward the door after Perkins and his struggling captive. Uncertain what to expect, he shoved the youth at a fast pace until they were clear of the doorway.

"Now boys, you can stay out and cool off or get your heads knocked together. Am I clear?" Cy demanded.

"Yes sir," came their joint answer.

Vince didn't blame them. Perkins was a formidable man to tell someone something and not have his orders obeyed.

"Everyone back inside. The fight's over," Perkins announced and the crowd turned back to the yellow light of the schoolhouse Shoot, Vince, they weren't hard to get out were they?"

"No, if it don't get worse than this I'll be glad to help." Both men laughed as they went inside and went their separate ways.

May met him and smiled. "You're part of them, I'd say."

"I think so," he said, taking her hand and prepared to waltz. He might just become one of them. They both were and that pleased him more.

Later that night, in their bed covers beneath the stars, the schoolyard full of campers had finally quieted in the wee hours. A baby's cries sliced the silence.

"We'll have that sound at our house come spring," she whispered.

"Sounds good."

"What are you thinking?"

"Oh, folks are a little edgy. The range is becoming more crowded. I just heard a few words tonight but I'm afraid there will be hard feelings in the future."

"Don't worry about that." She snuggled against him. "In a few months, I'll be big as that woman at the dance tonight about to deliver. You better hold me while your arms are long enough."

FOURTEEN

Sunlight flooded the kitchen. Seated at the table, Juan and Vince waited for their breakfast. "We better go round up the cattle down in the basin and get them up here," Vince announced.

May turned from her cooking at the stove. "Today?"

"We need to do it shortly. We don't have a lot of time before winter."

Juan agreed with a nod as she put pancakes on their plates. "Soon the wind will howl."

May wrinkled her nose at the prospect of cold weather. He silently agreed with her appraisal of the change of seasons.

"Can you ride down there with us?" he asked her.

"Certainly. I'm no invalid."

He studied her for just a moment, wondering if it would be best. If there was another way. . . .

"Stop worrying. I am not some kind of porcelain doll. I can ride from here to hell and back."

Vince saw Juan hide his amusement at her words. So he was the only one in this outfit that worried. Someone needed to be concerned. That was settled. He'd go hire the Holms boy to watch the place, milk, and feed the chickens while they were gone. Better safe than sorry.

Two days later, in the cool morning air, they left, trailing two packhorses loaded down with supplies. The freckle-faced youth rode his pony a ways with them, then he parted, assuring Vince he'd handle it all until they returned.

The third day they crossed the Verde. Vince deliberately held the pace down to keep from making her overly tired. On the west bank, May dismounted and removed her squaw boots to wade in the water. She washed her face with hands full of water.

"Someone's coming," she pointed as Vince adjusted the girth on the black. May hurried from the stream, seating herself on the ground to replace her boots. He could see the dust rising above the cactus and brush. Who was it?

Instinctive he switched the six-gun in the

171

holster around on his hip and flipped off the rawhide lace trigger guard.

"Who is it?" she asked, joining him out of breath.

"Papagos," he said, sharing a private look of reassurance and a nod with Juan.

"Horseman, you come back," the chief John Mendoza said, riding up on his coughing, sweaty horse.

Vince did not miss the man's hard appraisal of Juan or the woman. "What do the Papagos do for the Army these days?"

"Catch plenty bronco Apaches," the chief grinned. "Army pays twenty-five dollars for them."

"Sounds like high prices," Vince said.

"Plenty," the chief said as the other three tribesmen settled around him on their horses. "We got two this time." He held up the gunnysack that was tied to his saddle horn.

"Good." Cold chills went down his arms as he realized the burlap bag contained two heads. "We're taking my cows to the mountains."

"Who are you?" One of the Papagos crowded his horse in close to Juan's.

"Juan Lopez. What business is it of yours?"

"Where are you from?" the Papago asked, his eyes hard as coalchunks.

172

"Tucson."

"I'll vouch for him," Vince interceded, his hand on the Colt's wood handle. The sun's warmth on the wood felt hot in his palm. Would they challenge him?

"Lots of breeds rode with the Apaches," the chief said without apology as Juan's accuser backed down.

"The man is with me," Vince reiterated. The muscles in his chest were taut as a bowstring. If the Papagos wanted war, then he was ready.

"We will meet again, Horseman." The words were a threat. The chief reined his horse around. "You too, Lopez."

Filled with anger, Vince merely nodded as he faced the cold looks of the other Papagos filing by him. They were not satisfied. He felt certain that they knew Juan was a bronco. The knowledge of their discovery curdled his stomach as he watched the Indians cross the river. They would bear closer watching.

"What can we do?" she asked in a stage whisper.

"Get our cattle and go back. They have no proof that Juan is a bronco. Besides, who can tell a damn thing from a head?"

"A head?" she asked aghast. "They had human heads in that sack?"

173

"Yes."

"Oh, that's disgusting," she said as Vince helped her up in the saddle. He watched the line of scouts fade into the chaparral. Would they report Juan to the army?

"What do you think?" Juan asked.

"They can go to hell for my part," Vince said, swinging in the saddle. "But we'll be careful."

Juan nodded somberly.

"Keep that Spencer handy. They aren't likely to start anything unless they can win it easy."

"I can't believe the army pays for heads," May said as they rode up the mountain.

"They do," Vince said, and looked again for any sign of them on the break side of the river. There was nothing, not even a trace of dust.

In the sundown's scarlet glare, they rode into his camp. The sharp stab of disappointment stabbed him when he dismounted. The shade tarp was nearly gone, tatters slapping in the rising wind. The tent looked about to fall in. A place went down fast without folks using it.

"Jerky for supper," she announced. "If there's enough fuel I'll make coffee . . ."

Vince whirled. "What's wrong?"

Speechless, May pointed her finger. Two

young Indians were seated on their haunches in the greasewood. Perfectly still, they looked poised as the wind tossed the tails of their cotton breechclouts.

"Juan!" Vince called, not taking his eyes from them. "Get up here." Neither youth moved, and they appeared unarmed.

His man spoke to them in Apache. They nodded and the older of the two spoke to him.

"They're hungry," he translated, "and afraid the Papagos will find and kill them."

"What can we do?" May asked, searching around.

"Get out some of your jerky. Juan, tell them we will watch for them."

The *vaquero* spoke again and the pair seemed relieved. They did not move, even when Juan handed them a handful of the brown jerky. He noticed how they ate as if afraid someone would take the food away from them.

"Their names are Johnny Teller and Mark Badheart," Juan said. "They want to go to San Carlos where they have people but fear the Papagos will find them before they can get across there and kill them for the reward."

"What can we do?" she asked, concern etched in her eyes as she tried without suc-

175

cess to start the fire in the wind.

"I'll think of something," Vince assured her, kneeling to start the blaze in her kindling. Like he didn't have enough damn problems. The pair of wide-eyed boys in their mid-teens hardly looked dangerous enough to kill for a twenty-five dollar reward apiece.

Without a word, Juan took the Spencer and left them in the growing darkness. The Papagos would not be back for a few days if they went in the Brakes. That would give Vince time to locate his cows and get headed back for the mountains. What should he do with the pair? Maybe an Army patrol would come by? But worse, what if the Papagos followed him back to camp instead of going into the Brakes?

"I gave each of them a blanket," she announced. "They refused more food."

"Guess you got them fed and put up." He reached out and hugged her shoulder.

"How did they get out here anyway?" May asked.

"Damned if I know, but it's one more thing to look after."

"Are you mad?" she asked in a small voice.

"I'm not mad at you. Or anything that you've done."

"Oh, you'll think of something you can do

176

for their safety," she tried to reassure him.

Vince was grateful she was so certain that he could just do anything. He blew on the hot coffee. He felt boxed in. Two more Apaches were out there sleeping in his blankets under a Papago death threat. The scouts were not through with Juan either. His hired man was in as great a danger.

She'd seated herself beside him, hugging his arm, assuring him. "In the morning you'll have a plan."

He hoped she was right.

Morning came like a soft velvet grey kitten crawling up the horizon. Vince stood beside the quiet cottonwood without a breeze to rustle the leaves. His sleep-denied eyes searched the desert beyond the tule lined tank. Vince shifted the Spencer to his other arm. He needed to buy another long gun, so they had two. Stiff from sitting up all night in the cool air, he gratefully accepted her fresh coffee.

"What's wrong?" she asked.

"They're out there." Ever since he'd awakened, he had known the Indians were close by.

"Who?" she asked in a whisper.

"The Papago scouts."

"Why?"

"They want those bounties. They may not

know the boys are here, but I think they intend to add Juan to their list."

"You're making me sick."

"Sorry. You go back and start saddling the horses. Get those boys to help you. They can each ride a packhorse. We'll make a run for the store."

"Store?" she asked.

"A friend of mine, Pick Walters, has one south of here. I thought you went by it."

"Not here. I never saw a store close to here. There's one north of New Field, where I bought some food."

"Get going." He cocked the rifle. When the time came, maybe he could scare the scouts away with some gunfire. But in his heart he doubted that would work. Juan was searching north of the tank for any signs of them.

Vince shook his head. Their time was short. They needed to get moving and head for Pick's store.

He retreated cautiously to the horses. May and the two Apaches were hurriedly saddling stock.

"Did you see them?" Vince asked when Juan rushed in to join them.

"Yes, they've left their horses out in the desert. They're slipping in on foot. We will have time to ride." Juan glanced apprehensively over his shoulder.

"Mount up." Vince boosted her in the saddle with a grimace. He didn't give a damn about his own chances. He just hated to have her in the middle of the fracas when the shooting started.

A shot shattered the air. A pistol round, Vince surmised, booting his rifle in the saddle scabbard and surveying the others mounting up. He pointed south to May and slapped her horse on the rump to make it go.

His Colt in his hand, Vince fired at the first figure coming along the edge of some head-high greasewood bushes. The man was smoking away with a handgun. The distance was too great for effective shooting.

More of the scouts began to emerge.

Vince swung in the saddle and turned the black after the others, who were already out of sight.

If Juan knew correctly, the Papagos would be a while getting to their horses. The lead might be all they needed. The big horse surged down the dry wash. The dust of the others hung like a curtain in the still air. They were still not in his sight. They had a good start. If they could maintain it to Pick's store — the better cared for horses should out distance the Papagos.

Vince glanced back and saw nothing save dust and chaparral. The race was on.

FIFTEEN

The telltale dust of the trailing Papagos rose above the stalwart cactus behind him as he swung off the black.

"Vince Wagner, what the hell's going on?" Pick asked as the two Apache youths drug the horses by their bridles to the corral.

"I'll explain later. May, get in the store. Now!" Vince ordered. "Pick, break out some guns and ammunition. The damn Papago scouts have gone on the warpath."

"Warpath?" Pick sounded bewildered.

"Get inside. They'll come in here shooting their damn heads off. They're mad as hornets." Vince herded everyone for the doorway.

"I never heard of such —"

"Now's no time to argue."

A shot cracked the air. Pick realized the time to talk was later.

Off-handed, Vince slung four shots in the direction of the scouts as they rode up. Then

181

he hurried after the others into the security of the adobe store. Two bullets ricocheted off the door casing and Pick's ire showed.

"Why, that's John Mendoza out there," Pick shouted. "What the hell's wrong with those Indians? And who's she?"

"My wife. May, meet Pick Walters."

"Nice to — she's the woman? I'll be a son of a bitch." More shots pounded the adobe walls and broke Pick's amazement. "They mean business."

"Juan, take the back door. Tell this pair of boys to sit on the floor. May, you do the same." Vince shook his head to deny her unspoken offer of assistance. He wanted her out of harm's way.

A glass shattered above them, showering down shards as a Papago's bullet found the high side window. Vince ducked, listening to Pick swear as he loaded a new Winchester rifle.

"I've spent all my damn life worried about Apaches attacking and here I'm protecting two of them."

"Horseman," a voice outside called as the gunfire stilled.

"The chief," Vince said, straining to hear.

"Give us the two Apaches. Our fight is not with you."

"No!" Vince shouted. "I'll take them back

myself first. You're not killing these boys."

"We can trade," the chief said. "The black horse for them?"

Vince's heart stopped. Those red-bellied cowards would kill his black horse to get the pair. Horses meant nothing to an Indian, but they knew how much he treasured the animal. He clearly visualized the gelding in the corral.

"What are you going to do?" May asked. Flush-faced, she sat on the floor with her back to the counter.

"They want war, they'll get it. If they shoot my black, they'll pay."

"Oh Vince, can't you reason with them?" May pleaded.

Pick shook his head. "They're too worked up. I've never heard them talk like this before."

"The damn cave killing and the Army put them up to this headhunting business. They've killed all Chato's Apaches and now they're determined to annihilate the rest." Vince dared look out the door, the Winchester's stock pressed against his cheek.

He shouted at them, "You kill that black horse, I'll find you and I'll put you with your ancestors!"

The chief's voice came from the vicinity of the adobe ruins of a shed just past the corral and windmill. Some of the others hid in the lacey cover of a few mesquites. They'd reached a standoff. What bothered him the most was they had his horse in close gun range. But the store was fortification enough they couldn't storm it without suffering losses.

Vince's answer for the Papagos was a barrage of shots. A few of their bullets blistered the plaster near the doorway in response. Dust churned in the front door. Angered by their answer, Vince deliberately took aim, shot, and saw one of the Papagos go to crawling for cover behind the ruins as his fast-levered shots stung the dust around the man like wasps.

Juan's rifle sounded at the back of the store. Then silence.

"How many are back there?" Pick asked from his post at the high window behind the counter.

"One was," Juan replied.

"You get him?"

"He's hit."

"That means he's got less than a handful left to fight." Vince turned his ear to listen to the retreating drum of a horse. "He's sending for more help. Damn his red ass any way."

"Maybe I can go talk to him," Pick offered.

"Yes, and get your butt blown off." Vince took aim, and with two shots, chipped some adobe off the edge of the shed's wall. "He don't intend to talk to no one."

"How long will it take them to get back here with help?" May asked.

Vince considered her seated on the floor. "Couple of hours to as long as a day."

"What can I do?" She pushed herself up. "I'll get everyone some water."

"Just keep down," he said, alarmed she was moving around. But he realized short of tying her up with a rope, he'd never get he'd to stay in one safe place.

"I'll be careful," she pledged, busy filling a cup from the ojla hanging in the nest of ropes.

"Have you got a plan Vince?" Pick asked.

"If they don't get reinforcements by dark, we'll take them."

"And if they do?"

"We'll have a lot more damn Indians to fight." Vince shook his head. He couldn't make out a thing moving around the ruins.

"Here have a drink." She offered him the gourd dipper. "Do you think they'll get sensible about this?"

"No, I think the whole matter is out of

185

proportion. I've known those Indians out there for five years, they never acted hostile before."

"But now they are."

"Yes, ma'am, and I'm not certain, but they either want to win or die."

"What will happen to us?" she asked.

"You go sit somewhere safe."

Vince whirled as the two Apaches youths began to chant. It was a hopeless moan that made no sense.

"What is that?" May said.

"Death song, I reckon. I've never heard it. Have you, Pick?"

"No, but they can quit that squalling any time." The storekeeper ruefully shook his head.

"Juan! Tell them to stop. No one will die if they listen. The Papagos know that song, they'll only be encouraged."

"Besides, it makes my skin crawl," May protested.

Juan came and angrily ordered the pair to quit, and then he moved them closer to his outpost at the back of the store.

"It bothered me too." Pick climbed down from his observatory on top of the flour barrel and took the gourd from her. "I can't believe that my best friend found you and never told me the truth." The storekeeper shook his head as he appraised her.

"Have those men in the bowler hats been back again?" she asked.

"Yes, and they were very mad when they found the empty grave. Figured something was amiss then."

"You didn't need to know," Vince said, taking a break and pressing his back to the wall to rest his tired muscles. "The girl from the saloon, she's dead."

"And you're?" Pick asked her.

"May Wagner."

"Nice to meet you Missus Wagoner." Pick shook his head as if eaten with envy.

Sweat ran down Vince's temples. His gaze set on the area of the corral, the buckhorn sights on the Winchester ready to scan any movement. Where were they? He could hear the throat-filled howls of death. Could the Chief's messenger get reinforcements back by dark?

The air in the store was hot and fogged with acrid gun smoke. He doubted the messenger could ride that fast. But still there was a chance. For years these people had farmed and never caused a problem. For two scalps, they were giving up their long peace.

He longed to be home with May in the mountains where the cool winds blew. To enjoy her body in a feather bed, instead of worrying about peaceful Indians gone berserk.

The first rifle report brought him to action. The black horse screamed in pain. They'd shot him. All reason left Vince. He burst out the door, the loaded Winchester clamped in his vise-like grip. He raced across the open bare yard to the corral, oblivious to the shots being fired around him or even May's shrill protests. Vince Wagner was a man out of control.

Sixteen

Gunsmoke burned Vince's eyes as he advanced on the shed ruins. The Winchester held hard against his hip, he ripped off gunshots. The bullets ricocheted with a whine. He stalked to the corral. His breath rose and fell with each footstep while anger seared his mind. The Papagos had senselessly shot his best horse. He wanted them all dead.

Beyond the ruins, he heard them struggling to mount their horses. Realizing they were escaping, he ran to cut off their retreat. The rifle empty, he dropped it and freed his Colt. His lower lip twitched with rage as he ran by the corral. They were going to pay dearly for murdering the black gelding.

"Hold up, you horse killers!" he shouted as they whipped their horses to leave.

His pistol shots at the fleeing Indians were futile. Finally the hammer fell on empty casings, his arm wearily dropped to his side.

No use, they were gone. His failure to avenge the horse's death and their escape left him depleted. Vince closed his burned eyes and the pistol in his hand felt like a great anchor.

"Vince!" May cried, rushing with her skirt and petticoats in her hands. At least he still had May. Her winsome beauty encouraged him in his darkest moment. The effort of her running made Vince realize there were more important things than the black horse's demise. But he couldn't just wipe away his loss. He dreaded more having to face the matter close at hand.

He holstered the gun and caught her in his arms.

"Thank God, you're all right." Pale faced and out of wind, she gasped for air.

"I'm fine. Just bitter as hell at them." He held her ripe body against his own and shook his head. They'd pay for what they did. He studied the desert that had already swallowed them.

"Guess all they needed was to get you mad," Pick said, looking around for any dead Indians. "I just knew they'd gun you down."

"Stay with Pick," Vince said to May, apprehensive about his next obligation. Juan had already gone in the corral. He'd seen him slip through the bars. The report of the pistol told Vince all he needed to know. The black horse no longer suffered.

"Vince," she began, the concern for his loss etched in her handsome face. "I'm a big girl and I know what that black horse meant to us. I'm coming along."

He could not bring himself to deny her joining him. May had become a major part of his life, more than he even had admitted to himself. Whatever they possessed was as much her effort as his.

"Me too," Pick spoke up. "There ain't no live or dead Papagos left out here."

"That damn bunch of Papagos is going to think about bounty hunting a long time before they tangle with us again." Vince scowled again in the direction of their retreat. Even his worse violent profanity could not define the horse killers.

Blood traced from the black horse's velvet nostrils. Vince took a place on his haunches to study the wavy black mane and the silky hide floured with dust as the black reposed in death. The sleek carbon-black coat shone in sharp contrast to the scarlet wounds on his side.

The damn Indians didn't even know how to kill a horse. No, they had deliberately wanted the black in pain to get him to come out and expose himself. It was their intention then to pick him off, but they had lacked the guts to stay in the face of his fury and broke ranks for their horses. Damn cowards.

He closed his eyes. They were too dry to cry. He felt May's comforting hand on his shoulder.

"One day," she said with a quake in her voice, "you'll find another horse as great."

"I'm sorry *amigo*," Juan said. "This horse was like a brother when you had no one. I have watched you chase the wild ones. Such speed and power, no other horse could match him. You were like the wind, a part of him."

"You Apaches watched me?"

"Yes, many times near the Verde river we saw you."

"I never knew that."

"We wondered why you never had a woman and always lived alone. We went around your camp. Some of my people thought you were a spirit or a messenger."

"Like the boys from your camp that took May?" Vince asked.

"What do boys fear but fear itself? They wanted to prove themselves. To take such a woman seemed a big feat for young boys."

"It was." Vince rose slowly to his feet and

consider the task. "I want to bury the black."

"We're all going to help you," Pick said. "Juan, have those two boys go get some shovels and a couple of picks from the store."

Vince never argued with them. He watched the sun setting in the west, in the direction of New Field. Where were Allison's thugs? They'd be back.

"Thanks," Vince finally said to his friend.

"You'll really thank us when we get him covered up," Pick said. "I've done a lot of stupid things in my life but never had a funeral for a damned horse." The storekeeper shook his head as the two Apaches returned with the tools and the process began.

May served them supper when the pit was waist deep. Her bacon, beans, hoecakes, and coffee livened the men up.

It wasn't until after he'd finished eating that Vince remembered to reload his pistol. Then he went to fetch the Winchester. The muscles in his back were stiffer than they'd been in a long time, and the ground they were digging in seemed unforgivingly hard. Blisters on his hands began to ache. May joined him as he walked back in the twilight with the long gun.

"You're making good progress on the

grave," she said.

"I wish we were through," he said.

"It'll be cooler at the ranch." May tried to face the fresh night wind.

"Are you all right? I mean the baby."

"That baby's fine," she said to dismiss his concerns.

"Good." He headed for the others. Pick had set up a couple of lamps so they could see in the darkness. Both Apaches did their share, as if anxious to please their saviors. Vince felt good working. Another few hours would see the job completed. No amount of concern or being mad would bring the big horse back. That chapter in his life was over.

When they finished, Pick insisted Vince and May take his bed inside the store. He hung a hammock between two mesquites to join Juan and the Apaches.

In the bed, Vince felt the soreness in his muscles against the cotton mattress. Overhead, the shadowy light glanced off the goods and utensils hanging from the rafters cast patterns on the ceiling.

"It won't be long till morning," she said, raising up on her elbow in the darkness.

"No, but I'll sure sleep better when we get home."

"Did you ever dream about this? I don't mean losing the black horse, but how things

194

have turned out for us?"

He reached up and pulled her onto his chest. "No, and I don't want anything to happen to us either."

"In my life, I've thought I'd die a couple of times. I think I've stared death in the very face. I thought a lot about hell. But I never figured I'd ever want to live in a farm house and have a husband who did that."

She snuggled up close against him as he fell asleep.

The next morning, a brown hen fluffed and dusted herself beneath the mesquite tree. Her morning dry bath complete, she shook with fury and a small cloud of dust boiled from her. Then, preening her tail feathers with her beak, she prepared herself for the hot day ahead. A few yards away, watching her ritual, Vince sat on his haunches with Juan. They solemnly discussed the young Apaches and what they should do about them.

"Take them back with us," Juan said. "Then we can get them to San Carlos and never cross the Papago's land."

Vince considered Juan's idea. "You're probably right. We need to get home."

"Shall we leave today?"

"Yes. May seems all right to travel. We should be able to gather the cows as we go.

The boys and I can herd them. You better scout ahead for the Papagos. We get across the Verde, they're not likely to follow us."

Juan nodded. "Should we get our supplies we left at your old place?"

"No, the Papagos probably have those. We better buy some from Pick."

"Did I hear my name being used?" the storekeeper asked, squatting down beside them.

"We'll need supplies," Vince said. "I want to get started back today."

"I sell them, but your credit is still good."

"We'll pay. What about you? Will you be all right here alone?"

"Fine. I've been here ten years and plan to live a lot longer." Pick removed his glasses and shook his head slowly. "I can't believe that woman of yours."

"What about her?"

"She's a perfect lady. And she's making breakfast right now."

"She does that all the time," Vince said with a grin.

"You've got to be the luckiest guy in the whole damn territory. Find a dance hall girl in the middle of the damn desert and she turns into a wife. I just can't believe it." They laughed and helped each other up to answer her call. The food was ready.

"Pick." Vince said. "I never kept her a secret on purpose. It was only so you wouldn't be threatened by those hard cases."

"I know, you'd never seen her if I'd found her first. But I figure those round hat bastards ain't through looking for her. I kinda wondered myself when they came around the first time. Then I didn't think about you and the girl, but I'm sure they've added it up."

"I know they have." He glanced back over his shoulder to the west and the direction of New Field. Allison's killers no doubt had their minds made up. He needed to get moving and put more distance between them and her.

The cattle drive under way, the small herd raised a trailing cloud of dust whose telltale sign irritated and disgusted Vince. Even at a slow pace, their cloven hooves seemed to turn up enough loose granules for the sharp hot wind to swirl it skyward. They were marking their retreat. Despite having Juan out ahead searching for an ambush, they were sending big messages of their movement to anyone who wanted to know.

"What's wrong?" May shouted as she herded a reluctant calf back to the bunch.

"We've got to stop and rest." Vince wiped

his sweaty forehead on the shirtsleeve.

"But we're only a half day from the river," May protested, looking perplexed.

"It's the dust. They can see it for ten miles or more."

"What'll we do?" She raised the canvas water bag from her saddle horn for a drink.

"Find some Palo Verdes for shade and stop till dark."

She nodded. He set out to try his hand at explaining stop to the Apache boys. After two attempts, they finally understood him. In a circling motion with much effort by the three of them, the bunch of cows and calves finally halted on an alkali flat. There was the shelter of a cluster of pale green Palo Verdes or they could just stand in the sun. The great roan bull dropped heavily to his front knees, then settled in with a grunt that made up the rangy cows' minds this was a rest.

The two Apaches slipped off their horses and used their animal's shade to hunker down and watch the herd. Vince nodded his approval at them and went to join May. She'd found another shade tree for herself not too distant from the cattle.

"Will this work?" She stared out across the desert's vastness.

"It has to." He drank cool water from the

sweaty canvas bag and returned it.

"Your friend Pick was jealous, did you know that?"

"Did you want to stay at the store with him?"

She whirled and frowned at him. "Of course not."

Vince laughed. "Anyone would be jealous of me having you."

"I'm not such a find." She shook her head as if he'd embarrassed her. "My reputation and past — what's wrong?" She blinked at him as he stared hard to the south.

"Rider or riders," he said, trying to see their dust again. He'd only caught a glimpse of it.

"Who is it?" Her face was flushed.

"It may be Juan." He hoped he was right. He couldn't be sure. Though he hated to scare her, he stepped to the saddle and eased the new Winchester out of the boot. When he levered a shell in the chamber, Vince heard her gasp.

SEVENTEEN

Three white men rode at the lead, trailed by four Indians. Their suits were floured with the desert powder, and their mounts looked jaded. Obviously the red men in the group were reservation policemen, and despite the heat, they wore heavy blue coats.

Vince held the rifle ready as he sized them up. Across the dry wash, the two Apache youths were already on their feet and looked about to mount up and ride at the first sign of trouble.

"Deputy US Marshal Hal Brooks," the leader said, holding his coat open to expose the silver star on his vest before letting it fall back. A full handlebar mustache under a too large nose, he had a hawkeyed look. Vince read him as a rough, tough individual.

"Vince Wagner. My wife, May. What's your business up here?"

"Several things. A couple of Papagos claim you shot at them."

"Shot at them —" May's face became red with anger.

Vince rode in and held his arm held out to signal to her that he would handle the lawman.

"We were attacked by some Papagos yesterday at first light," Vince said, studying lawman's poker face. "We had to ride at breakneck speed to Pick's store where they attacked us again and shot my best horse."

The lawman began nodding. "Pick shared the same information. Why in hell you figure they ran back to the agency and lied to their agent Mister Rose here?"

"So they wouldn't get in trouble for attacking us. How the hell should I know?"

Brooks nodded his head. "There is something wrong here, Wagner. There's never been a case of trouble with these Indians. You're saying you were attacked. They say they were attacked while picking saguaro fruit."

"Look at the saguaros around here. See any ripe fruit on them?" Vince asked.

"You've got a point." Brooks agreed.

"Did they show you the heads of the Apaches they had with them?'

"Nope." Brooks cast a frown back at the bespectacled man grasping the saddle horns. "Mister Rose, get up here."

In response the agent booted his horse forward, obviously not an experienced horse rider.

"Have them Papagos turned bounty hunter, Mister Rose?"

"I don't understand," the man said, very displeased at appearing to be the brunt of the lawman's inquiry.

"Mister Wagner said the Papagos are out headhunting for Apaches."

"Carmine! Do you know of such things?" Rose asked his assistant, the third white man, who Vince decided would look even more suited to be behind a desk.

"No sir. The Papagos are farmers and very thrifty people. They raise maize, beans, melons, and cotton."

"The hell with the horse crap," Brooks roared. "Were some of these Injuns that reported they were attacked out headhunting for Apaches?"

"I don't believe so," the secretary finally said.

"There's your answer," Rose said satisfied.

"The damn Army is paying them twenty-five bucks a head and they bragged on it," Vince said.

"Still that don't tell me why they attacked you," Brooks retorted pointedly.

"Those two San Carlos Apache boys," Vince said, motioning toward them. "I wouldn't let the Papagos have the boys to just kill."

Brook rubbed his cheek with his palm. "There's more here than meets the eye. Mister Rose, are you still wanting to press charges against this man?"

The Indian agent went blank for a moment. Vince wondered where Juan had positioned himself. He didn't need bloodshed with this bunch and May standing not three feet from him.

"I suppose we could ask the tribesmen involved again the true nature of their business." Rose sounded uncertain enough that Vince felt the matter might dissolve itself.

Brooks scowled at the man's wishy-washy answer.

"I'll be in touch, Wagner. Ma'am, I'm sorry but you look familiar. A young woman named Dailey I once knew." The lawman seemed to be trying hard to place her.

"Were you ever in Kansas?" May asked. "I was raised on a small farm."

"No ma'am, weren't no farm where I knew her from." He reined his horse around, then asked Vince, "What about those two Apaches?"

"I'll personally take them back to San

Carlos as soon as I get my cattle home." Hopefully that would satisfy the lawman. The three Indian policemen held dour looks of disinterest.

"Julie Dailey — damn, I never forget a name." The lawman shook his head as if the recollection pleased him. "But I'm sorry, ma'am, she'd never have made a rancher's wife. Go on Wagner, take them boys back and get them a pass if you work them. Mister Rose, you've got lots to learn about Indians and the Arizona Territory. . . ."

Vince didn't hear any more the lawman told the Indian agent. He nodded to reassure the two Apaches. Juan would be coming in as soon as they were out of sight.

"That no-good, low down, son of a bitch Brooks!" May swore, her blazing eyes mere slits as she glared after them. "He did that on purpose."

"No," Vince said, "he paid you a compliment. He said Julie Dailey would never make a rancher's wife."

"Nor would she ever escape her black past?" May whipped at her skirts with the bridle reins.

"You have with me. Mount up, we're pushing for home."

"*Sí, patrón,*" she said with a toss of her head.

204

Juan materialized from the dry wash and shook his head. "I was out front near the Verde. Sorry, but it was too late when I saw them coming."

"They weren't any great problem. I think between the Indian police and that marshal looking hard at those head hunters, we'll have a safe drive back to the mountains."

"It will be good to be in the mountains," Juan said with a wide grin. "We have a good place there."

Vince nodded agreement. He gazed after the thin column of dust Brooks and his posse stirred. Too close. He was grateful the lawman had only recognized her. After the war that man had once worked in Georgia. Vince remembered him.

"What's wrong?" she asked, moving her horse in beside him.

"Nothing, just glad we're headed home."

The plume of dust slowly faded on the wind. Like his past, he hoped.

EIGHTEEN

The moon rose over the sawtooth range to the east and joined a full crop of stars. Vince held his rifle close to his chest and listened to the coyotes howling on the high points. They were no threat to his small bunch of cattle and calves. His concern lay with two-legged varmints.

"The Papagos would never come this far," Juan said.

"We don't know that. They never operated as bounty hunters before, either. The Papagos or those two hired killers could have found out we were trailing cattle and followed us. We aren't making twenty miles a day."

"Do you think they are on our back trail?"

"I'm not certain they are or they ain't. But the hair on the back of my neck's been standing up like I know more than I do."

"First light, I'll slip back," Juan said. "You, May, and the boys can herd the cattle?"

206

"Yes, and a thousand more."

Juan laughed. "Johnny and Mark are good cowboys."

"They learn fast." Vince did appreciate the pair. A critter never quit the bunch that one of the youths wasn't herding them back. "Juan, you be careful."

"I will be gone in the morning."

"Like I said, just be careful."

"*Sí, patrón,*" They both laughed at the notion.

Vince listened hard. Was it only his imagination gone wild or did he really know something about their being pursued? Nothing in the night indicated a thing wrong and he finally went to join May in their bedroll.

"Is everything all right?" she asked sleepily.

"Oh, yes," he lied. "It's all right."

Dawn came like a pink paintbrush, slow at first. Just a wink of peach color, then the shadows grew in intensity. Vince and the boys were saddling horses. The cattle were up grazing the grama grass. The water in the wash had been another blessing, for they would be content for another day on the trail. Vince couldn't promise himself water holes every day in the journey, but so far he had found enough for the stock.

"Where's Juan?" May asked as she handed out plates of bacon and pancakes.

"Gone to check our back trail."

"I thought you said nothing was wrong." May glared at him as she handed him the tin plate.

"Can't be too careful. Between you and me, we've got plenty of enemies."

May shook her head in disapproval, then took a seat on a large rock. She hadn't spoken her piece on the matter, but if he told her his suspicions it would only further upset her. Times like these, a man never got it right. The meal was silent.

"I'll stay and wash these dishes," she said. "Then I'll pack up these things and catch up in an hour, as slow as the cattle go."

Vince wondered if he should let her do that. If he didn't she would berate him some more for not telling her everything and still he didn't feel it was safe. In the end he agreed to stave off an argument.

"You just don't dally around here. I'll expect you caught up with us in an hour. No longer."

"You sure are bossy as hell," she said under her breath, and began noisily slinging dishes and utensils into a cotton cloth she used to carry them to the water to wash them. "And you two bucks quit laughing."

She straightened up and shook her finger at them. "Haven't you ever seen an angry squaw before?"

Her outburst was too much for the Apache youths. Without a word, they fled to their horses, mounted up, and began gathering cattle.

Vince shook his head at her action. "You've scared my cowboys to hell and gone."

"Are you through with that cup, Mister Bossy?"

"You're sure pretty when you're mad," he said, handing it to her.

"Because I only have one hour," she said spitefully. Shouldering the dishes in the cotton cloth, she headed for the water hole.

Vince watched her. The dun and the packhorse were snubbed to the juniper. She would be all right. Besides, Juan was between them and any possible threat. He started shouting at the cattle to get them moving as the boys drove in the ones from farthest out. Vince counted his herd as they headed northward on the trail.

Satisfied with the tally, he gave the two Apache boys the signal to let the herd go. They were headed for the mountains that lay ahead. Towering like a great bulge in the earth, the tan bluffs and spotted conifer clad slopes meant they would be home in three days. Vince looked back. He could still see the dun and May's packhorse. She was out of sight doing the dishes in the waterhole. He'd be glad to be back home.

The trail swept down a wide grassy basin in a westward direction before it twisted north again and ascended the steep way up the front range. Vince wondered if they could reach the summit by dark.

Periodically he glanced over his shoulder, wondering about Juan and when May would catch up with them. He reined up the bay horse. The sun was too high. Where was she? He rode over and spoke to the two Apaches boys.

"I'm going back." Vince pointed in the direction they came from.

Both boys nodded as if awaiting more words.

"Keep going on the trail." He pointed at the well-beaten path and the direction they were headed.

They nodded again.

Vince could do no more with his cowboys. They understood quite well what their job was. He set spurs to the horse and short-loped him back toward camp.

Where was May? Probably digging up some flowers for her yard — he urged the horse on faster. She should have already caught up with them.

Wet with sweat and grunting, Vince's horse climbed the rise with effort. On top, Vince reined the gelding up short. There was no sign of the dun or May's packhorse. Where had she gone? He twisted around, searching the brown grass valley for any sign of her. Had he missed her riding back?

She couldn't be far. He rode to the juniper where he last saw her horses hitched. Leaning over, he studied the dust. His discovery sickened him. There were unshod pony tracks mixed in the dust. Had the Papagos taken her? He vowed if anything — anyone harmed her, they'd pay dearly.

When he rose up, Vince licked his dry numb lower lip. What had they done with her? Why? For more revenge? He tried to see the new prints mixed in with the older cattle prints.

He halted the bay. Their apparent direction of travel was more southwest than south. The range they seemed headed for was unfamiliar to Vince. If Juan went south, he'd probably missed them. Damn, should he go get the two boys? They must be two hours away and whoever had May had a good head start. The Apache boys would have to figure it out by themselves. He put spurs to the horse.

The tracks were obvious, except on occasional hard rock-encrusted places. Vince had no problem following them. He kept an eye to the looming range, wondering if her captors knew these mountains. No time to worry about an ambush, he wanted her safe.

The entrance to the canyon was narrow, a notch in the looming, red sandstone face. Vince drew the Winchester out of the boot.

There was no sense being a damn fool. They had the edge, but the Papagos seemed to have little stomach for close-up fighting. Why did they take her? He shook his head, reining the horse around a great boulder in the dry creek bed. If this is a trap, they have me. He urged on his mount with his heels as he craned his head around to see what he could of the sheer walls hemming him in.

The air in the canyon became hotter, like a giant stove as the high sun's radiation broiled the confines. Sweat stung his eyes, making his vision hazy. He fought to clear them, rounding another sharp corner in the wash.

Rifles blazed like cannons in a tumultuous roar that threatened his eardrums. The bay reared, screaming in pain. Something tugged at his shirt as the horse spilled over

backwards —
 Vince's world went black.

NINETEEN

His headache hurt the worst. Vince tried to rise up, the hammering inside his skull like giant drums. Darkness engulfed the canyon. Someone was with him. He tried to focus on who was there. He recognized the butt of the Spencer rifle that someone beside squatted beside him held. Was Juan there? In the darkness and his grogginess he could not tell.

Then he recognized Johnny and Mark. The Apache boys looked at him with great concern. Even in the starlight they appeared afraid. They're probably worried about night ghosts, Vince decided. With great effort he managed to sit up.

How long had he been there? And — damn, they were gone with May.

"Have you boys seen Juan?" he managed to ask, discovering with his fingers that a bullet had furrowed the side of his head. The tenderness and mass of scabs formed told him he had been out for a while.

"Juan?" he asked, staring into their faces under the starlight.

"No Juan." Mark shook his head. "Juan *muerte.*"

"Someone killed Juan?" Vince could hardly believe his ears. Both boys gave solemn nods.

Vince looked away. How had they ever killed the former Apache?

"Huh-uh," Mark grunted for Vince's attention. Then held the side of his hand to his throat and made a sawing motion.

"Those bastards decapitated him?" Vince wanted to shutter. The no-good devils that did such an act deserved no mercy.

Vince worked his legs. Sore but useable. There were no other wounds besides the one on his head. Damn, Juan was murdered, May captive, and he had two boys that didn't savvy ten words of English and damn little Spanish.

Shakily, Vince pushed himself to his feet. The youths acted ready to steady him if he needed any help. His legs felt like spindly branches. Damn, if the bullet had been a quarter inch over he'd be with Juan.

"Help me on the horse," he said indicating the first pony.

"Wait for sun," Mark said.

215

"They'll be to hell and gone by then. There's no ghosts, just me." Vince felt for his holster and the empty sleeve drew a frown. Had he lost it?

"My pistol. Look for it," he said, searching in the starlit sand of the wash.

"Huh," Mark said, handing him the gun, a trail of grit streaming from it.

No time to clean it. Vince shut his eyes against the pounding in his head. He hoped the pain would stop, but doubted that it ever would. The swing up on the pony was tough and he forced himself to wait until the dizziness stopped.

"Tonto gringo," Mark said in disapproval and pulled his cohort up behind him on the other horse.

"Go find my squaw," Vince said, hoping they savvied all of it. "Get May."

"May," Mark said. Then he booted their horse and started up the dark canyon like the sun was shining. Vince took some pride in the boy's confidence, because he knew Apaches dreaded night worse than little children. At the horse's first movement beneath him, he caught his breath with the sharp pain in his side. Something else was wrong. No matter. He had to find May.

Vince desperately fought his headache and the pain in his hip, side, and chest. He grit-

216

ted his teeth to stay on the horse cat-hopping up the mountain behind the two Apaches. He wished he'd taken his saddle from the slain bay rather than riding bare-back, but that would have taken valuable time.

How much lead time did the kidnappers have? He must have lain unconscious half the night. The loyal boys had come back for him. They'd found poor Juan murdered. He clenched his jaw at the thought the bastards had decapitated him. A wonder the pair stayed after finding Juan. He held the mane tight in his fist as the horse jolted him, charging up a loose rockslide. Under his scrambling hooves, the animal spun free of the talus, sending it rattling off the sheer wall and avalanching down the steep canyon's sides for hundreds of feet.

The horses were blowing so hard Vince wished the pair would let them catch their breath at the summit. He also wanted to rest, but wasn't about to complain. Mark seemed to know the way, though, and when he saw Vince was on top, he piled their horses over the crest and off the downside.

Vince swallowed hard. This was broken malapi country. An Apache would know it like the back of his hand. Despite his attempts to match silhouetted peaks with ones

217

he knew, nothing was familiar. He hoped the pair ahead knew more than he did. Besides, in his condition, he was lucky to be alive and able to ride.

He glanced eastward and saw the morning star. Still could be hours till dawn. There was no hint of it on the far horizon. Vince clung to the hank of mane and tried to stay on the horse as they made the steep descent. *May, I'm coming.*

Vince blinked his eyes. He was no longer riding. The boys had him propped up his back on the side of the wash. They must be off the mountain. Mark gave him a palm full of water. With great effort, Vince forced the small amount of liquid down his constricted throat.

Had he blacked out? He couldn't recall, except he felt weaker and wondered how close they were to the kidnappers.

"I'm all right," he lied, forcing himself to sit up as if nothing happened.

"Johnny," Mark pointed at his friend and then at himself. He held up three fingers before Vince's eyes. "Papagos!"

"The Papagos are over there?" Vince pointed. "Is May over there?"

"No May. Vamoose," Mark said, with a wave of his hands.

"Two *gringos*?" Vince asked. He held up

218

two fingers, considering Allison's gunmen.

"Uno gringo." Mark banished one digit.

Vince was struck by the notion only one of the killers had come with the scouts. Who the hell was it? Had Allison himself hired the Papagos to take them up and cross this range for the element of surprise? But if it was not Allison, which was it?

"Round hat gringo?" he asked.

Mark shook his head, no. "Go get Papagos. Pistol?"

He wanted Vince's pistol. They had Juan's Spencer. Vince wanted to confront the Papagos himself. He owed that to Juan, but he knew how badly the pair wished to avenge their tribesman's death.

The headache grew worse. Vince wondered if he would die in the mountains. Every muscle in his body ached. He twisted slowly and drew out the Colt, then handed it butt first to Johnny as the light of dawn peeped over the wall above them. Johnny nodded in appreciation. What could he say?

He closed his eyes and hugged himself in the coolness of the canyon. The two Apaches were gone. If they were killed, he would probably die in the next two days. Should the Papagos survive, they might kill him if they came out this way. Vince settled back on the hard dirt, no matter, he was so tired. . . .

Screams hurt his eardrums. Yelling, shooting, and the dust churned up in the street.
Vince was riding the black horse, snapping
shots at other men rushing from building to
building. He drove the black in an alleyway
to reload. A dove in a low cut red dress
leaned out the window and waved a lacey
kerchief at him.

"Come up here after you kill them —"

"May! May!" Vince woke up shouting. The
sunlight burned his eyes. The boys weren't
back and he'd been dreaming about her.
His breath came in short gasps that knifed
his lungs. Where the hell was the pair of
Apaches? He strained his ears but only
heard a distant crow calling.

How far was the water? Maybe he could
crawl there. With much effort he pushed
himself to a sitting position. His head
stopped gyrating. He pulled his knees under
him and tried to rise. Things began to swirl
and he caught himself on his palms.

"Give me strength," he prayed aloud. The
dizziness abated and he crawled toward the
wash, hopeful there was a seep or small pool
of liquid.

But he found nothing except the bleached
grey rocks lining the arroyo. He closed his
eyes and let himself face down in the dirt.

He had a jackknife. How far to a barrel cactus?

On his side, Vince tried to focus his blurry vision on the vegetation around him. Not much, a few straggly greasewood bushes, a large patch of prickly pear. He began to crawl on all fours. There had to be a barrel cactus.

Twice he fainted in his quest, recovered, and crawled on. The palms of his hands stuck with the tiny spines that littered the desert floor. Finally, he saw a small, squat cactus and at last lay on his side next to the succulent. Carefully he studied the fishhook barbed ribs. The plant was well fortified.

He drew out his knife, opened the blade with great effort, and began to plug the cactus. Juices ran down from his incision and made his dry tongue press against the roof of his mouth.

The cactus pulp tasted warm and with an alkali slackness but the moisture gave him strength. He removed another piece and chewed on it. Was the cactus poisoning him? His head began to swirl and he fainted again.

He could never keep the situation straight. He woke riding on a travois litter and the two Apache boys on their own horses. Johnny was on a bald-faced horse that looked familiar. Where were they taking him? He had been unconscious so much he could hardly remember days and nights. Where was May and the one gringo? How many days had they been moving? Vince wished he knew more.

"Who shot you?" the white man asked, awakening Vince. He found himself in a bed with a roof above. The pounding in his head had stopped — had he gone mad?

"Renegade Indians. Where's Mark and Johnny?" Vince demanded.

"They're probably showing off for some young maiden," the man said, rising with a white porcelain pan and the wet rags in his hands.

"You the doc?"

"Unfortunately yes. I'm Doctor Hayes. And you are very lucky to be alive. Mister . . . ?"

"Vince Wagner. Those two boys saved my life." His head was bandaged and he was undressed under the sheets. Someone had scrubbed him up, no doubt after days on the trail — Vince didn't want to think about it.

"Doc Hayes," the man repeated and started to leave him.

"Doc, wait, I need some information."

"What?"

"Where the hell am I?"

"San Carlos Agency. What else?"

"When the hell can I get out of here?"

"A week or two if you rest and eat what they bring you."

"Yes." Slumped back in the bed, all he could think was how her kidnapper could take her anywhere, even kill her in that length of time. Sunlight glared on the west window of the hospital. He accepted the food tray the short, thickset Mexican woman brought him.

"*Señor,* you must sit up very carefully," she fussed about him.

"I will," he said to appease her.

"They say you shot three Papago headhunters in the mountains after they gave you that bad wound."

He nodded. Mark and Johnny did not want the blame for it, he decided. But a white man who was attacked could do that. He recalled the bald-face horse Johnny had ridden. The pair had avenged him in his own name.

"Are you all right, *Señor*?"

"Yes, *Señora,* I will be all right."

She looked into his eyes. "How you ever lived coming so far. I wonder if you saw the Virgin during that time."

"Who?"

"Our Virgin Mary?" The woman waited for his answer.

"She may have heard my prayer," he said to be respectful. "I did not see her."

The woman crossed herself and bowed her head. "I am sure she held your hand." Then she left him.

An orange-red spear of light came in the west window and shown on the floor. He wondered about May. Where had she been taken? He must eat and regain his strength. Carefully, he spooned in some of the beans. He needed a divine hand to help him.

TWENTY

The checkers and the board blurred. If he could only shake his head and clear his vision. He didn't want to admit to Doc Hayes, but at times, his vision was still impaired. This game of pretense forced him to sit on the edge of the cot and concentrate when he actually wanted to sleep away more of the weariness that persisted in gripping his body and mind.

"You're tired and can't see very well," the physician said, puffing on his pipe.

"I'll make it, Doc," Vince said, to scoff away any advice the medical man had.

"Well, you damn sure won't beat me at checkers making moves like that." Doc collected two more of Vince's red pieces.

Both men looked up when Maria entered. She glanced from him to Doc and back as if she was uncertain how to begin.

"Well woman, what's wrong?" Doc asked in his gruff sounding voice.

225

"There's a woman — I mean a girl to see *Señor* Wagner."

"Good. I'll get out of here. Any woman come to see him would be better company than me beating the pants off him at checkers."

The older man rose with effort and shook his head. "I think you're lots better Vince. Head injuries are strange. They take time to heal. You aren't having those bad headaches are you?" Doc looked over his glasses at him.

"No." Vince was grateful they had ceased. But this must be day eight of his stay in the small agency hospital at San Carlos. Every waking moment he was eaten with anxiety about May, but frustrated by his lack of strength, too weak to even consider riding a horse. Everything he planned seemed put off by his affliction and the lingering effect of the gunshot wound that had grazed his skull.

"Show her in," he told the waiting Maria.

When the young Apache woman hesitated in the doorway, he waved the girl closer. Dressed in a brown blouse and skirt with many layers of slips beneath, she came and stood before him. Maria had gauged her age closely. The girl must be in her late teens. Handsome, though, with pride in her carriage, Vince judged her to be old enough to be an Apache wife.

"My name is Betty Red Stocking."

"I'm Vince Wagner. Have a seat, Betty Red Stocking." He indicated the chair Doc had vacated.

She refused his chair offer with a head-shake. "I do not need to sit. I come to speak for Martin and Johnny. They do not speak English."

"Yes, I know that. Are they all right?" Vince had wondered about the pair and what had become of them since their return.

"They're fine. They've searched hard for your woman. May?"

"Yes, my wife. Have they found her?" Vince felt a surge of new energy, brought on by the girl's words.

She looked around as if unsure to continue.

"Maria is all right," he said to reassure her. "She is probably eavesdropping but don't worry."

"The white man took her to Tucson. Mark and Johnny tried to free her but could not. Then he took her to Goldfield."

Goldfield was less than two days' ride from his bed. Vince considered how risky their actions were on his behalf. Dangerous enough for them to be off the reservation,

227

let alone mess with a killer. "They have taken much risk. Was she alive? All right?"

Betty nodded her head. "They are afraid to go there alone. They fear the Papagos might catch them around Goldfield."

"I understand. You get each one passes so they can go with me. Tell them over at the agency they will be cowboys on my ranch. I spoke to the agent this week and he knows all about that."

Hesitantly, she repeated the word. "Passes for cowboys?"

Vince studied the floor and wondered if they knew the name of the person who held his wife. But he decided they probably had no way to know since they spoke so little English. He looked up again at the girl.

"The agent will give them passes for such jobs. Also have them buy a buckboard and a team for me to ride."

A small frown formed on her smooth face. "They have extra horses."

"I get dizzy. Better not chance riding a horse. In the morning, we'll go."

Vince rummaged in his pants pockets for the money.

"Can they get guns?" he asked softly.

She nodded quickly. "They have plenty of guns."

He placed five twenty-dollar gold pieces

in her palm, then looked in her brown eyes. "Is this enough to buy it?"

"Plenty. In the morning we come with buckboard." She smiled broadly as if her mission had been a success. He watched her disappear.

Vince settled back. Those two Apache boys had done their damndest to get May free, scouting to Tucson. Why did he take her to Tucson? Didn't sound like he intended to kill her. The boys had taken a great chance by even going there. At least May was still alive. He gave a grateful sigh. Thank God.

The early morning sun shone on the buckboard parked outside the hospital's front porch. Johnny Teller waited on the spring seat holding the reins. Mark Bad Heart rode the bald-face horse and Betty Red Stocking sat the other saddle horse. Vince nodded to them. Obviously she also had gotten some kind of a pass for herself. Whatever. The threesome eagerly shared his readiness to recover May from the hands of her captor.

"Vince, I sure hate to see you go," Doc Hayes said, pumping his hand. "I'll sure miss those checker games. Take care of that head. Any sort of a blow could give you worse headaches than you've had."

Vince agreed and thanked the army surgeon. Then he hugged Maria Gonzales, the sweet housekeeper who had tended his recovery.

"I will always be indebted to you, Maria."

"Oh, *Señor* Vince, I know you will find your wife," she said, on the verge of tears. "The Virgin Mary will help you and I will pray for your success."

"That will be help enough." Vince stepped up in the buckboard. From the seat, he barely issued goodbye and Johnny clucked to the fresh team. They were off. Vince turned back to wave at the pair. But he doubted from the dust they ever saw his gesture.

At Florence that evening, they stabled the horses. The first day had worn him down worse than he would admit even to himself. Vince took in a hotel room while the Apaches stayed at the wagon yard. Grateful for the bed, he fell across it still dressed and went to sleep without even eating supper.

The next morning, he awoke with hunger pains. Gradually he drove the haziness from his mind while seated on the edge of the bed. Was he a match for Allison? For any of them? Had he taken a fool's way to suicide? His wits certainly were not as sharp as they needed to be to meet cold blooded killers face-on.

In the hotel restaurant, he ordered break-fast. Grateful for the strong coffee that revived him, he was a full day's drive from Goldfield. Perhaps in that time he could regain more of his senses and strength. He wished May knew he was coming for her. She'd probably given up on him being alive, thinking the Papagos had killed him.

The Gila River was slack with late summer's diminished flow and hardly seemed capable of floating the waiting ferry. The ride across the stream started uneventfully. Betty, the experienced one, gave orders to the Apache on how to load the buckboard and horses. Mark, Vince decided, was the one who must have the claim on Betty. But besides his insight, his helpers appeared to be very alert and ready for anything.

"Guess you and these bucks are going to Goldfield, huh?" the operator asked as he guided the chugging, steam powered side-wheeler toward the north bank. An older man, his clothes were ill-fitted and pants too short and exposing part of his bare calves as well as his unlaced shoes.

"I guess," Vince said idly, not interested in the man's small talk.

"I had a man and a woman on here two days ago. Lucky Clover Murphy —"

Vince sprung at the operator, wadding the man's shirt in his fist. "Who did you say?"

"Hey, let go of me! You gone mad?" The man looked affronted at Vince. Both boys had their guns drawn and pointed at him. "Lucky Clover Murphy. For God sake what's wrong with you guys?"

Slowly, Vince released his hold on the man's shirt. "What did the woman with him look like?"

"Fancy woman. Yes, she was a looker. I won't forget that. Light brown hair. Real short in a school girl kinda bob."

"Where was this Lucky Clover going?"

"Goldfield, he told me. What did he do to you?"

"The woman, did you hear her name?"

"Julie, he called her."

"That woman is my wife." Vince said, staring overboard at the muddy water swirling lazily around the ferry. "He and some hired Indians tried to kill me and kidnapped her."

"Damn, Mister, how the hell was I supposed to know that?" The man fussed with his shirt, tucking it back in front. "Come to think of it, he didn't look none too happy."

"Two days ago?" Vince reiterated. She was still alive. The news gratified him. LC, not Allison, had hired the Indians, which solved another mystery for him. Where in the Hell

232

had Murphy taken her?

"Yeah. Guess I'd get uptight too if someone took my woman and she was that pretty." The ferryman straightened his poor posture and glanced around apprehensively at the two Indian boys, who had holstered their weapons.

The bow struck the sandy landing and both Apaches led the team off the boat. Betty brought the saddle animals. But Vince noticed her dark eyes watched the operator like a hawk.

"Goldfield? They said they were going there?" Vince asked the man again. "Anything else you heard?"

The ferry operator shrugged, "That's what he said."

"Thanks." Vince crawled up on the buckboard. If they hurried, they'd reach Goldfield in a few hours. How in hell's name did LC ever get her? He nodded his approval when Johnny slapped the team to go faster.

The chaparral flew by, and without pausing, they passed the stage stop at Florence Junction. Headed northwest on the Mesa-Phoenix road, the team raced without persuasion. To his right, the dark wall of Peralta Range rose above the giant saguaros and catclaw thickets.

Vince closed his eyes. In a few hours, they

would be in Goldfield. If the team didn't die. He wanted to face her abductor and have the matter settled. Far to the north, beyond the peaks over the Brakes, they had a ranch to share. They had their lives to live. He glanced at the intense youngster driving the racing team, who in turn nodded in understanding at him. They were going to get May. And do it quickly.

The midafternoon streets of Goldfield were deserted when Johnny reined up the sweaty team and let Vince off. The Gold Palace Saloon across the hard caliche street caught Vince's eye.

He checked the .44's load. Satisfied with the gun, he motioned for Betty to ride over. The lathered horses were breathing hard.

"Betty, have them cool the horses and then water them. My business won't take long. I'll find him and get her. Take good care of the horses."

"We will be close, if you need us," Betty said, booting her horse off to the rig. The boys listened to her orders, but they seemed almost unwilling to leave him alone in the deserted street.

"I'll be all right," he said. "Cool off the horses."

She spoke to them again in Apache and they left him. Vince wondered as he watched them go out of sight if he looked pale. They certainly acted concerned about his well-being. He'd be fine. The adrenalin in his system from knowing May was close by would sustain him.

His heartbeat increased as he strode to the Palace's porch. If LC was anywhere, he'd probably be gambling at the Gold Palace, which looked to Vince from outward appearances as the richest game in town. Someone stepped out the swinging doors and Vince stopped with his hand on the butt of his .44. A ruffled white shirt, striped pants and a stovepipe hat, the individual on the porch was a gambler by his attire. Was this LC Murphy?

"You ain't looking for me," the man said with a shake of his head. He held his hands out to demonstrate he had no notion of going for a gun.

"Are you LC Murphy?" Vince's eyes narrowed, and despite the mid-day heat, a cold chill swept the skin on his back.

"No, my name's Gunther Tharp. I damn sure ain't that four-flushing son of a bitch Murphy either."

"Is he in there?" Vince asked, indicating the Palace.

"Nope, he's probably sleeping off a hangover in the back of Swain's store."

"Where's the woman he brought here?"

"Which one?" Tharp grinned as if he knew of a dozen Murphy kept.

"The one he brought here a day or so ago."

The man shook his head. "He didn't have a woman with him last night."

Vince grew angry. Was the man lying to him to protect Murphy?

He turned at the sound of a struggle. From between two buildings, the two Apaches wrestled with a red-faced man in a rumpled white shirt. Strong-armed between them, they brought him.

"Let go of me you damn heathen redskins!" the man protested.

"There's your man, LC himself." Tharp laughed and moved away.

"This is *gringo*!" Mark said and shoved him toward Vince.

There was no doubt for Vince. This was Murphy who hired Mendoza and the bounty hunters as well as kidnapped May. The boys knew him on sight, for they had trailed him to Tucson to try and free her.

"LC Murphy!" Vince shouted. His chest muscles trembled with the rage consuming him as he considered the gambler.

"Who's asking?" LC sounded inebriated. He stood a little unsteadily as he straightened his rumpled frilly shirt.

"Where's Julie Dailey?" Vince grabbed Murphy's arm and jammed the .44 muzzle under his weak chin.

"She left me. That no good bitch. I rescued her from the damn Indians and she left me," he slurred, still sounding drunk.

"You brought her here?" Vince demanded.

"Yeah and she left me the first night. I should have whipped her harder. That bitch —"

Enraged at the man's words, Vince slugged him on the head with the butt of his pistol. The gambler sagged to his knees, crying and protesting. Vince intended to show the filthy-mouthed dredge of society what whippings were about. Using the Colt's barrel for a weapon, he struck again and again at Murphy until his arm tired.

Then, out of breath, Vince rose up and holstered the pistol. At his feet, the whimpering gambler lay face down in the street.

"If I ever set my eyes on you again, I'll hang you, Murphy," Vince snarled. "That's a promise I'll keep. Arizona ain't big enough for the both of us."

His headache was back as he bent over. The glare of the sun hurt his vision as he straightened and replaced his hat. He had lost it sometime during the disturbance. The boys, their weapons drawn, looked around, as if expecting some sort of intervention from the townspeople.

He tried to focus his eyes. A few onlookers stood on the Palace's porch. None of them looked like the law or ready to come the aid of the moaning Murphy. Vince wanted to kick him for good measure, but decided better.

Where had she gone? West, surely. Were their drawn guns still necessary?

Still they were taking no chances. He wished he had more strength and his head would stop thundering inside.

"Hee yah!" Betty screamed as she whipped the team up to a sliding stop beside him. "Get in."

The boys took the saddle horses tied to the tailgate and mounted them.

"Your woman left the night before on horseback," she said, giving him a pull by the vest to hurry him. "I spoke to an old Indian woman who saw her leave."

Vince nodded that he had heard her. Without looking again at the gambler, he settled in the seat beside her. In a fury of rein slapping, with Betty screaming at the team, they left Goldfield.

Where had May gone? Vince's world wanted to darken. His hand tightly gripped the iron grillwork on the side of the seat. Vince felt Betty steady him with a hold of her arm around his shoulders.

Gradually his head began to clear, but the numb throbbing persisted.

They were halfway to Mesa when Vince considered going north to Pick Walters's store. May might retrace that route to find Pick or even Juan, if she suspected him alive. Phoenix, she'd probably avoid, knowing LC would trail her there. Vince looked over his shoulder for signs of pursuit. Nothing save his two cowboys loping their mounts. He pointed for Betty to take a dim road headed north through the catclaw and cactus. She expertly wheeled the buckboard that direction.

In late afternoon, they forded the shallow Salado River below one of the brush diversion dams used for irrigation. Vince wanted to let the horses rest and blow, so he walked along the stream bank to wear out some of his frustrations. Shaken by his own intentions to slay Murphy by pistol-whipping him to death, he wondered if he would go mad before he located her.

By dusk, with the sun stretched far to the west, Betty topped the last rise. The small adobe store and windmill of Pick's place sat before them in the midst of the grey-brown desert. With a mite of grandeur, the Apache maiden expertly swung the buckboard in a large arc that spewed dust in a great cloud. She brought the rig to a halt before the door.

Vince dismounted, searched around before heading into the entrance. "Pick? Pick, where the hell are you?"

Something was amiss. The chairs at the table were toppled on the floor. Vince's hand closed on the butt of his Colt. Where was Pick? Had May been there? His eyes adjusted to the room's shadowy darkness. Was this a trap?

A distinct moan came from behind the counter and he rushed to see. Pistol in his hand, he peered over and saw Pick Walter sprawled on the floor. In disbelief he blinked at the storekeeper's shirt and apron crimson with blood. He'd been shot up.

In a fluid leap, Vince vaulted over the counter and beside his friend. Damn, who'd done this to him?

The whine of a bullet sent a small spray of adobe into the room.

"Who in the hell's shooting?" Vince demanded as he tried to comfort his semi-conscious friend.

Johnny spoke sharply in Apache.

"He says two white men," Betty said, translating for the boys.

240

Vince stood up with a scowl. What the hell did they want?

Both boys stood back from the doorway. With rifles in hand, Mark and Johnny both nodded. That meant Allison's hired guns were outside.

"Betty, tell one of them to guard the back door," Vince ordered, "and you come help me make Pick comfortable."

There were more shots, but they were ineffective. His friend was badly wounded, too bad to probably live. The least he could do was make Pick comfortable with a blanket under his head and one to keep him warm.

"Vince?" Pick spoke so softly Vince was forced to lean close.

"I think they hired a boy to warn them . . . that May was here. He hung out here . . . for weeks. Always had a little money to buy his food . . . and never did any work that I knew about." Pick closed his eyes as if straining for more strength. "Guess I should have knowm the little rat was spying on me . . . and waiting for her return."

"Did they take her?"

"Yes. But it was my fault —" A fit of coughing broke off Pick's words.

"Don't blame yourself," Vince said. "I should have settled with Allison and his

241

guns a long time ago."

"Who's . . . she?" Pick blinked his eyes in disbelief as Betty knelt on the other side of him

"Betty Red Stocking. Mark Bad Heart's wife or about to be." He smiled. His friend still recognized a pretty woman even bad shot up. "Hold his hand," Vince told her.

Anything to comfort Pick. He'd probably be dead in a short while. Outside, there were more bursts of gunfire.

Vince joined Johnny at the front door. They both hugged the wall as the sporadic gunshots splintered the door casing.

"Can you go around them?" He made a circling sign with his hand.

Johnny repeated the movement and nodded.

"I'll do plenty shooting. You *elcanjo*?" Vince said.

The boy grinned at being called a jackrabbit.

"We've got you surrounded, come out with your hands high!" one of the gunman ordered.

"Why don't you go to hell?" he shouted back. The caller was close. Probably lying on his belly this side of the corral.

Vince needed a loaded rifle. He intended to make it so hot on the caller he was forced back to the ruins. From the rack he took a new rifle, spilled a box of cartridges on the counter, and began cramming shells in the magazine. The shots rapped on the windows and door openings

Beside the front door, he drew a deep breath.

"Go!" Vince shouted to Johnny poised by the rear door, and then he stepped to the left of the front entrance, pouring hot lead in a flurry.

The rifle empty, he deftly stepped back out of the way. The man he'd shot at on the ground near the corral had been hit. Through the thick gun smoke, Vince saw him roll over in pain. The other was answering his shooting. Several slugs slapped the thick adobe wall.

Vince coughed on the thick fog of bitter gun smoke but his ear was attuned to what the gunmen outside were saying. He heard nothing to indicate they had noticed the Apache slip out the back way. With a quick grateful prayer of his own, he thought of Maria and hoped the kind soul did lots of praying for them. Maybe burn a candle in the chapel. They would need all the help they could get before these hard cases would give up.

"You ain't getting away this time!"

That voice might belong to Red Mills. Vince felt certain Dimer had been the victim of the gunfire he'd laid down. The acrid smoke forced him to cough again. Reloading the rifle, he sat on the floor to escape the black cloud in the store.

"Come, your friend is dying," Betty said softly.

Half sick to his stomach, Vince rose and followed her behind the counter. He sat on his haunches, wishing he could do something more for his friend.

"May told me you were dead," Pick managed.

"Why did she think that? Save your strength. We're getting you out of here and to a Doc I know."

Pick shook his head. "Get those bastards for me —"

Slowly, the light of life's lamp began to slip away from Pick's green eyes. Vince saw it ebb lower and lower. Powerless to stop the action, he watched his friend die before him. He licked his dust-bitter lips and then met Betty's brown-eyed questioning gaze.

Wordless from the thick constriction in his throat, he pulled the blanket over Pick's face. There were killers to deal with. The Kii-yii-ing screams outside and the thunder of horse hooves meant one thing. Betty nodded at Vince.

Johnny had begun his attack by separating the gunmen from their mounts. The gunmen, realizing their losses, were swearing after the boy, though not a shot was fired. Vince bet Johnny had been riding low. The Apache knew a white man would never shoot at a horse to stop them.

"Let's talk trade!" Vince shouted. "Your horses for your guns and you leaving here."

He settled down on the floor as the front door buzzed with bullets as his reply. He shrugged and shook his head.

"I thought my idea was a good one," he said.

Betty joined him, holding a rifle. "I can watch the back door. You want Mark to go help Johnny?"

"Not yet. We're dealing with real stupid gunmen out there. They can't walk back to New Field in their boots. But they may have to unless they trade for their horses back." He cupped his mouth. "We're ready to negotiate about transportation fellows."

"Go to hell in there!"

"I promise you won't have to walk to New Field if you give up. Come dark, thirty of them Apaches will be shooting arrows at you."

"You're crazy. One gawdamn Apache buck

took them horses."

"Sure," Vince shouted, "but he's gone back for more bucks."

"We'll blow them off the face of the earth."

"I'd sure hate to die like that," Vince said.

"Cut the crap. Come out with your hands up."

Vince closed his eyes. He needed Red out of action to end the siege. Obviously Dimer was down. Where were they holding May? With a shake of his head, he drew a deep breath. One gunman to go. Time for him to take action. Filled with resolve, he pushed himself to his feet.

In a crouch, he burst out the door, firing his Colt in the general direction of the ruins where Red must be taking cover. A second gun joined him and he realized that Johnny must be shooting at the gunman too.

"Hold your fire!" Red shouted in disgust.

"Hands high and get out here!" Vince shouted.

"Dimer's shot in the leg," Red said. The big man's arms were raised high.

"Well, you get out and tell Dimer to start crawling or he's buzzard bait for the Apaches."

"Hey," Red shouted, "you ain't handing us over to them."

Vince crossed the open space to the corral, wary of any possible tricks.

"Where's May?" he demanded from Red. Dimer was on the ground moaning about his wounded leg.

"New Field," Red said.

"What the hell did you come back here for?"

"That's for you to figure —"

"Give me your *cuchillo,*" Vince said to Johnny, who held his rifle on the pair.

Deftly, the Apache tossed the thick-bladed dirk to Vince.

"You want me to carve your damn heart out?" Balanced in his palm, Vince looked from the knife to Red.

"She's there." The gunman scowled and shook his head.

"Where?" Vince demanded.

"Allison's got her at the Lucky King mine."

"Why did you come back here?" Vince asked.

Red glanced around as if considering his possible escape. "We came back to finish off the storekeeper, so he couldn't talk."

"You did a good job on him," Vince said, wondering if there was a tree tall enough to hang the two.

"I'm hit bad," Dimer whined, clasping his

hand over the bleeding wound in his upper leg.

"You'll live long enough to hang," Vince said, still resisting the idea of lynching them on the spot. If they implicated Allison in the murder, then he'd have witnesses. The big man wouldn't be easy to convict in court with his money and power. Vince decided to take them to New Field.

"Watch them," Vince said to Johnny and headed back toward the store.

Betty and Mark met him halfway.

"Johnny has them covered. We'll wrap up Pick's body, then we can come back later and bury him. We need to close up the store. May is at New Field and Allison may have already killed her."

"What can we do with them?" Betty asked as they hurried back to the building.

"Put them in jail and let the white man's law settle it." She in turn told Mark something in Apache. He agreed with a nod.

New Field was another hard day's drive, perhaps longer. Vince worried about May's safety. How long would Allison let her live?

Both of the outlaws' hands and feet bound in ropes, they rode at the rear. Betty drove the buckboard with her usual skill. Few men could match her driving. Even Johnny lacked her ability to corner it in such a turn that the wagon slid in a half-circle. The setting sun glared them face on as they pushed westward.

Vince's head pounded in time with his heart. He didn't like to think this run might be futile and May might already be dead.

The stage stop's yellow lamps shown in the silver moonlit desert. Their horses were winded, and his own belly complained. This would be a place to rest a few hours and find some food.

"We'll stop here and rest," he told Betty. The young woman drew the weary team to a halt and Vince dismounted.

"Good evening," the sleepy Mexican woman greeted them. Clutching a colorful shawl about her thin shoulders, she eyed them suspiciously from the doorway.

"My men need some food and our horses need a rest."

"They are Indians," she said with a curl in her lip. "They must eat out here."

"Fine, bring us out food," he said, searching around as Mark and Johnny uncinched their hard blowing horses.

"What about us?" Red grumbled.

She'd probably let them inside, Vince decided. "Shut up, you're lucky to be alive."

"*Señor?*" a grey haired Mexican man asked, finishing dressing as he came outside.

"My wife says you want food?"

"Yes, we have ridden far and have prisoners for the law."

"Outlaws?" the man asked, squinting to see the two, but not daring to leave the security of his porch. "*Madre de Dios.* But I'm sorry, the rules say no Indians in the dining room."

"Just bring us food," Vince said.

"And us?" Red shouted.

"I suppose so," Vince said. "Mister, Red will pay for all this. Maybe pay you a double eagle if you'll hurry."

"Oh, *Señor,* we are so glad to have you here," the man said, and retreated inside the house.

"What the hell are you talking about Wagner?" Red demanded, holding his tied hands out to be undone.

Vince ignored his wishes. "I figure where you're going money won't count anyway. So you can pay for this. Where's your money?"

Red scowled and shook his head in a black rage. "You son of —"

"You want to eat or not?" Vince asked.

"It's in my vest pocket." Red dropped his head in defeat.

"Good," Vince pulled out a leather purse and hefted it. "Thanks."

"Go to hell," Red mumbled after him.

Vince leaned against the porch post and studied the desert beyond. For supper, the beans were spicy and the meat stringy, but he hadn't realized just how hungry he had become. They probably fed the same food to white people. New strength began to surge in his body and the headache subsided.

"Where is the Royal King mine?" he asked the station keeper.

"A little ways, you turn north. The road where you turn off is marked. The mine is six or seven miles from the stage road up in the foothills, Maybe eight miles. You got business there?"

Vince nodded. He glanced over as Red hollered for more food. The big man held out his plate for the woman to refill it. Both killers were still bound by their feet and seated in the back of the wagon. Red might take a chance, but not one he'd lose in the blink of an eye and be dead. Johnny watched the pair carefully while Betty and Mark sat on the bench against the wall and ate their meal together.

They were still several hours from where Allison held May prisoner. But they did have the element of surprise. How long had it been since he'd seen her? Slowly he exhaled. If anything had happened to her, he'd kill Allison with his bare hands.

Finally underway, Vince wondered how long until dawn. The clock at the stage station had chimed three o'clock before they left. In three hours, the mine shift would close

At the base of the hills, Vince sent Mark ahead to scout for the mine. Unfamiliar with the area, Vince felt certain an Apache could learn all they needed to know. Paused in the dry wash, away from the road in case someone came by, they waited in the cool night air.

"When you have your woman will you go back to the place in the mountains?" Betty asked.

"Yes. When I have her safe and these men in jail."

"Mark and Johnny wanted me to ask if they can go there."

"And you, too?" Vince smiled at her.

She nodded. "San Carlos is not a good place. Apaches belong in the mountains."

"You can live on my ranch and your children too."

She blushed in the moonlight. There was a horse coming down the mountain. Vince heard the hoofbeats on the gravel. Too soon for Matt's return —

"Help! Goddamnit, it's Red —" The hired

gunman's outburst cut off.

Vince frowned. He'd heard the clunk. Johnny obviously had silenced the gunman with his rifle butt. But who was riding up? Colt in hand, Vince ran over to some boulders short of the road.

The rider called out. "Who's out there?"

"Get off that horse slow, mister," Vince ordered, unable to see much more than an outline against the sky. "Real slow and careful."

"That you, Red?" the voice asked, uncertain.

"Hands high," Vince ordered.

"Who the hell are you?" the man growled as Vince jerked his gun out. Betty caught the horse and Vince herded the man back to the wash.

Obviously this man had not seen Mark on the trail.

"You work for Allison?" Vince asked.

"Listen you son of a bitch — you can't get away with this."

"Is the girl still there?"

"What girl?"

Vince jammed the gun hard in his back, causing him to stagger a few feet ahead. "Where's Allison keeping her?"

"In the damn tool shed. Who the hell are you?"

Relieved to learn May was still alive, he pushed the man on.

"Welcome to our party," Vince said as they approached the buckboard. "We got Red and Dimer, now you can join them. They're going to hang for murdering Pick Walters. You can swing with them."

"Hang? Are you crazy? I ain't done nothing."

"Kidnapping a woman for ransom."

"Hell, that's Allison's deal," the man protested. "I just work as a mine guard."

"The judge can decide that. Tell Johnny to tie him up," Vince said to Betty. "I'm going to ride up there and see if I can find Mark."

"Johnny can watch them," she said. "I can help you."

He wasn't about to deny her assistance. She could match most men. "I'll take his horse."

"Can you ride?" she asked.

"Nothing could keep me from this," Vince said

The sun cracked the sky in a yellow burst over the hills beyond. Vince crouched behind the boulder with Betty. There was no sign of Mark. The mine consisted of an array of tents and some raw buildings. The day shift was harnessing mules to use on the mine carts. Vince pointed up the arroyo where they could be closer and perhaps decide which building was the tool shed.

They slipped carefully behind a large wood structure. Voices of the men walking by were clear.

"I'm going to take my pay."

"Oh, yeah. We'll see. Why that gal at —"

Vince searched around. This building concealing them must be the office or barracks. But across the tracks that led to the mine was another frame building, handy to the rails, which serviced the gaping mine entrance.

Betty tugged on his arm and indicated for them to get under the building. There would be ample room, for the structure sat on piers. Vince agreed. Besides, it would only be a matter of minutes until someone discovered the two of them standing in the open like this. Damn, how could they cover the hundred yards to the tool shed unobserved? They crawled under the structure.

"You stay here," Betty said softly. "I will go look in that building over there for her."

"Wait, what if they see you?"

"I am a woman. So what?"

"I don't like it." Vince shook his head as he bellied down beside her.

"And where is Mark?"

"Hey," someone shouted. "There's a damn blanket-ass buck out here wants a job."

Mark. Damn, they'd caught him. Vince pounded the ground with the side of his fist. The attention seemed to be centered behind them on the south side of the structure concealing them.

"Go," he said to Betty, and drew his Colt as they squirmed to crawl out. They wouldn't kill Mark right off. Besides they probably just thought he was snooping around looking to steal something.

Out of breath, they managed to reach the door. Betty turned with disappointment at the sight of the large padlock. Vince's skin crawled. No way to shoot it off and not draw a crowd. Betty pulled him around to the side and covered him with her body.

"What the hell's going on?" someone asked.

Without a word, Betty pressed herself up against Vince, holding his gun hand between them. Vince saw her intention was to make the man think they were lovers. She wiggled suggestively against Vince.

There were only seconds to act.

The mine employee's ham of a hand fell on her shoulder to pry them apart. "Who the hell —"

Vince's gun hand jabbed the muzzle in his belly. He spoke through his teeth. "Unlock that damn door or prepare to die."

Betty crowded close to both men to conceal the pistol. After a quick check around, she nodded to Vince.

"Who in the hell are you?" the red-faced man demanded as he undid his keys and began to undo the lock.

"You just better worry how you're going to live the next five seconds," Vince said, shoving the man inside ahead of him. "Where is she?"

"Who?"

He struck him over the ear with the gun barrel. "Your memory better improve quick. My patience and time is short."

Betty closed the door behind them and checked the window. She turned back with an all clear sign.

"Look in those side rooms," Vince said, jerking the man up on his toes. "Which one?"

"The trap door," the man gasped.

Vince wheeled him over. "Open it."

Shakily, the man complied and pulled up the door. Vince kept the gun hard in his stomach as he looked down in the cellar. "May is that you?"

"Yes, oh thank God," She scrambled up

the ladder and Vince caught her under his free arm.

"Thank God," he gasped.

"How did you find me?" she asked. "Oh Vince, when I heard your voice a minute ago my heart stopped. I thought you were dead." She was sobbing and shaking against him.

"The baby?" he asked hesitantly.

"He's tough." She managed a weary smile. "I still have him."

Vince nodded, relieved. He had her, and the baby was all right. "Get in the hole," he ordered the man. "One word and you're a dead duck. Hear me?"

"How do you figure to ever get out of here alive?"

"Blast my way," Vince said, looking at all the wooden boxes marked explosives. His prisoner inside, he bolted the trap door down and hugged May again to be certain she was all right. She looked very tired. But he was so exhilarated to have her again he knew she would recover.

"Open some of those boxes, we need to fuse some and set some others."

"Who is she?" May asked as he opened a stick at the end to arm it.

"Meet Betty Red Stocking. She's Mark and Johnny's partner. They've been trying

258

to get you free since LC took you."

"Thank you," May said. "They tried in Tucson, didn't they? Oh, Vince, I've missed you so. I just knew the Papagos hired had killed you like they ambushed Juan. Even bragged you were dead."

"I'm fine. We better worry about getting out of here. How does it look outside?" he asked Betty, who stood by the window.

"No sign of anyone."

"Here, May, you carry these explosives outside for me. Now, Betty, once these sticks start going off, you girls run for the horses. Don't look back. This place is going to really blow if they all go off. I'm going after Mark."

He lighted a three-stick bundle, and with the fuse spewing, ducked out the door and tossed it far under the main building. He lit another, reared back to throw it toward the mine entrance, then a second one with a lot longer cord in the same direction.

"Go," he pointed to the two women.

The explosion from under the building sent a force ripping out that nearly struck them down. Debris fell on the upper side. He watched Betty push May ahead. They were heading downhill toward where the horses were hidden.

Men were shouting and Vince slipped

around the building on the lower side with his pistol in hand, satisfied they'd gone around to see the damage. He had about reached the southwest side, where he expected to see Mark and his captors, when the next explosion near the mine entrance went off. He could hear the men shouting and cursing.

"Drop that gun," Vince ordered the lone guard holding Mark. The man obeyed, and Mark swept up the Winchester with a grin.

"Let's go this way. There's more explosions coming," Vince said with a head toss to the Apache. Mark needed no coaching.

The percussion of the second explosion hit their backs, but both men were running hard and far downhill. Vince glanced back at the great ball of dust. They would be in chaos for a while figuring out all the sources of his explosions and if there were more to come.

The women were already mounted on one horse, holding out the reins to a second one for them. Vince took the saddle and Mark swung up behind him. They bolted for the buckboard. No time to worry about Mark's horse. They needed to get to New Field and find the sheriff.

Relieved with his success at finding May alive and all of them escaping, he watched

May hugging the Indian girl's waist on the galloping horse. What if Allison owned the New Field law? He'd figure something out.

TWENTY-ONE

The adobe jailhouse bore the faded sign Cholla County Jail. Betty reined the buckboard up in front. Vince looked around the deserted main street of New Field. Two men, one wearing an apron, came out on the porch of a saloon and stared at them.

"Who the hell is that?" Vince heard one ask the other.

"Beats the hell out of me, but he's going to find the sheriff is long gone."

Long gone. The word rolled off Vince like big raindrops repelled by an oilskin.

"Who's the deputy sheriff?" he asked May, helping her off the rig.

"One of Allison's thugs," May said with a frown.

Red began to laugh on the back of the buckboard. "Well you got us here but you'll never put us in that jail." His contemptuous laughter only made Vince madder.

"May. You and Betty go to the telegraph

office and wire Tucson for US Marshall Hal Brooks. Tell him there is major public disorder at the mine and to come to New Field at once with several men."

Vince turned his back to the pair on the saloon porch and handed his pistol to the Indian girl. Turned away from the two men up the street, she slipped it inside her blouse and waist band.

"I'd send someone else, but the boys don't speak English," Vince said.

May looked him in the eye. "They won't lay a hand on us in the daylight. Come Betty, the telegraph office is only a half-block away."

"Red," Vince said softly. "You may think you're safe here, but I suggest you haul Dimer inside unless you want another clunk on the head, which I'll give you to shut your mouth. Understood? You too," he said to the third man.

Anxious for their success, Vince watched the women hurry up the far side of the street.

He drew a breath and motioned for Johnny to keep both girls in his sights so could he march the three prisoners inside. The tall youth drew his Winchester from the scabbard and leaned the barrel on the buckboard seat, ready to shoot. Vince hoped it wasn't necessary, but until the women were back he would have to rely on his coverage.

Inside the oven-hot jail, Vince frisked the threesome then locked them in the center cell. Behind bars, Dimer complained his leg was rotting off. Red just stood back as if contriving how he would settle the score with Vince when it was over. Vince saw the hatred and read the man's intentions. The third man, nonplussed, kept saying Allison would have them out in a matter of hours.

The cell door locked and checked, Vince nodded to Mark, and they hurried out front to see the girls hustling back. Johnny exchanged a worried look with Vince. Betty openly carried the Colt in her hand, and the two of them were walking as fast as they could. Something was wrong.

The situation was practically out of hand. Had they managed to send the message? Then a tall man in a suit with a high-crowned hat started from the saloon porch to intercept them. There was no mistaking his intentions. He was going to detain the pair. Vince took the rifle and aimed at the man's feet. A loud report and the sharp puff of dust beside his boot caused the man to whirl, his hand on his gun butt.

"If you intend to die gut-shot," Vince

warned with the sights bored on the stranger's brass belt buckle, "then draw, Mister. Otherwise, lift that pistol out real slow and drop it in the street."

"Who the hell are you?" the man demanded.

"The new law in this county until the federal officers get here."

Out of breath, May and Betty slipped around the buckboard.

"It took Betty and the pistol to make him send it," May said. "He wanted Kyle to see it first."

Vince nodded, motioned them toward the jailhouse door.

"Betty, tell Mark and John to vamoose for now. Go hide. I don't need all of us pinned in the jail."

She spoke to them in Apache. They quickly swung on their horses. Vince handed the rifle to Johnny. *"Vaya con Dios, amigos."*

The two boys looked a little lost but nodded to him and swung their horses around, He turned to offer Betty a chance to leave with them but she and May were already inside the jail.

Vince looked around. The shooting iron still lay in the street, but the out-of-sight owner obviously had found another. To clear out the front, he spooked the buckboard team away from the door and went inside.

The siege of the Cholla County jail had begun. One man, two women, and three prisoners . . . Vince wondered if he'd taken leave of all his senses.

"There's a barrel of water," May said, busy inventorying the supplies.

"Plenty of guns," Betty said, unlocking the chain through the trigger guard on the rack of Greeners and rifles.

Vince drew out the side drawer on the desk. "There's lots of ammunition."

"And several tins of food, some coffee, and lots of crackers," May said.

"Help me move this desk," Vince told the women. "I want to shoot out from that upper window if I need to." He indicated the eye-high, narrow portal made of glass bottles mortared in a row to emit light into the jail's office. "I think I can sweep the empty lot and most of the street from here."

"Should we close the steel shutters on the front windows?" May asked.

"Yes. Allison must know we're here by now. Wait. Listen."

A rider came pounding up the street. "Boys! Where's Mister Allison? Somebody attacked the mine this morning. They've got that Dailey woman and blew the hell out of everything."

"Allison ain't here."

Vince smiled. Left to their own wits, those idiots might take long enough to charge the jail that Hal Brooks would get there before then. But the reality that the lawman could be days getting there hung like an ominous cloud over Vince's head.

"Did I hear that man right?" May gasped.

"I heard him. Where would Allison go?"

"Wickenburg, Crown King. Who knows?" May said.

"We've got a chance. Between the mine and us, they may not figure two and two. It could split their forces."

"What about Mark and John?" May asked.

"They will do something to help us from out there," Betty assured her, returning to cramming ammunition in the long guns.

"You in the jail!" someone shouted. "I'm deputy Sheriff Joe Sales and you've got two minutes to come out with your hands up!"

"He's one of Allison's men," May hissed.

"We got a special order from the US Marshal's office to hold this jail. A trainload of lawmen will be here by dark," Vince shouted.

"Ha. Fat chance. He sent that telegram to Florence, not Tucson, so your marshal won't get it."

"Damn," Vince swore, and wiped his

267

sweat-beaded upper lip on his sleeve. "He may be lying. We ain't giving in that easy. Besides, I figure our lives ain't worth a plug nickel unless we hold this place."

Resolve in her brown eyes, Betty pushed the muzzle of a twelve-gauge through the slot in the wooden shutter, aimed, and fired. Knocked back by the recoil, she smiled at Sales's yowling as he fled for cover, obviously peppered with the shot. "Too much talk."

"How did you do that?" Standing beside Betty, May broke open the scattergun and extracted the brass casing.

She reloaded and snapped it shut. "Easy. Look down the middle of the barrel and pull the trigger."

"It will kick," Vince warned her, watching the street for more activity. Several men ran back and forth, wasting no time in crossing and keeping a wary eye on the jail.

"What are they doing out there?" May asked, hefting a shotgun and going through the motions of shooting it.

"Lady, they're planning how they're going to shoot and gut the three of you," Red said from his cell.

"Mills," Vince's voice a low growl. "You say one more word and you'll be wishing you'd kept quiet."

"I aim to use that squaw girl, when this is over." His face pressed against the bars, the leer on the gunman's face was so certain, so positive he would have his way.

"No." Vince shook his head and walked back in the cell portion. "If we don't live to get out of here neither will you. Mills, I'm saving my last bullet for you. But if you don't shut up I won't need to save it. Will I? You savvy?"

The gunman turned without a word and went back to the iron bunk. For the moment Vince had silenced the man. But he meant what he said. Mills and Dimer would never deny the executioner for killing his friend Pick Walters.

The jail grew hotter as the afternoon passed. Out on the street, men lugged several barrels to the end of the porches as shields for shooters to crouch behind. Vince watched them. Simple workers brought them and quickly ran away once their burden was dropped.

The positioning of the scattered barrels was not good enough to provide a fortification. But they did offer cover for a sniper.

"I'm going to stop this barrel business," Vince said, angry that the action continued.

"And shoot the poor unarmed men being forced to bring them?" May asked.

He took a single shot Remington down and examined the barrel. Definitely a rifle for accuracy. He loaded the long pointed cartridge in the chamber, drew over the latch, and cocked the hammer. A worker came out of the store a half-block away, a barrel on his shoulder. Vince took careful aim at the center band of oakum rope. He squeezed the trigger and the rifle's report echoed in the buildings. The explosion of flour dust from the busted barrel covered everyone nearby. Many fought their way into the street to escape the fog.

"Good shooting," May said, impressed.

A wide smile spread across the Indian girl's face. "I hope those boys saw that."

"They'll figure out some things on their own," Vince said, drawing a deep breath and taking a half-ladle of water from the jar.

"Listen, you in the jail! We know who you are. You've only got two women to help you. Better send them out. We won't hurt them."

May drew in a deep shuddering breath and jammed the shotgun through the slot. "You're liars! Allison locked me in a dungeon." She lowered her voice as she peered out the peek hole in the shutter. "I can't see who's yelling at us."

"The corner of the building across the street," he directed from his peep hole in the steel front door. "Peel some paint off there. He's close to it."

Vince smiled when the blast from the gun backed her up, but with resolve she clicked on the other hammer as two men rushed away from the smoldering siding. She fired the second barrel.

Both men danced away and then screamed going out of sight, obviously burned by some of her pellets.

"They can come back for some more," he said as May reloaded the shotgun under Betty's guidance and congratulations.

"Do you think they'll charge the jail?" May asked, sitting on the floor.

"They might do anything. We'll just be ready."

Betty rested in their desk chair with the Greener over her lap. Her hair was wet with perspiration. Rivulets ran down her temples.

"It's all amounted to nervy fun, now they know we can shoot. They won't come too close. We took their guts away."

Betty slumped to the floor and sat with her back to the desk. "Is it cool at your ranch?"

"Oh, yes." May sighed heavily. "Much cooler than this."

Vince sat on the cot and silently agreed.

Much cooler than this place. He shut his eyes.

"Cowboy! You and them squaws got ten minutes to come out with your hands up or I'm riddling that jail full of bullets."

Vince was on his feet to check out the front window's rifle slots. Damn, he silently swore. On the lot across the street, they were hand-moving a large Conestoga wagon in place.

"War wagon," he said grimly.

"Listen, that's Kyle Allison's voice," May said. "I'd know it anywhere."

"Now you can sweat, cowboy," Mills said from the jail.

"Shut up!" Vince ordered. He had to think. His head pounded as he tried to plan his options. If the end came in a crummy little territorial jail, he just hated the fact he and May didn't have more time together. They were so close to having a life together.

"Get down low," he said to the two of them. "They'll run out of shells before they totally destroy this building. The thick walls would take a few cannon charges."

The gunfire began. Bullets by the hundreds poured in, pockmarking the wood shutters and rapping on the steel door. The dust billowed up in the room. Vince quickly took the jar down and hid the precious water container under the desk. With May under one arm and Betty the other, they huddled on the floor waiting for the shooting to stop.

When the guns finally silenced, Vince was on his feet. Five men with long guns were coming abreast from the lot. They came as fearless as if they knew everyone in the jail was silenced and destroyed.

"Get a shotgun apiece," Vince whispered, hoping the prisoners could not hear him. "One chance to shoot and be accurate. Betty, you take the two on the left, I'll get the middle two. May get the right one and turn on the remaining ones. Shoot both barrels, then drop quick, because they'll really shoot at us, once we down five of their men."

Vince rose and barely dared to watch the line of men. They had reached the street, making small talk as they came, flashing the rifles at their sides. Building bravado as they came. He took his scattergun from Betty and moved to the steel door.

"Don't put the guns up until they're in the middle of the street," he said quietly. Five more feet, he could hear them talking and their soles scuffing in the grit.

"Now!" he ordered.

The three guns' double blasts were deafening. Arms flew up, men screamed, some turned but too late. All were cut down. Vince squatted after he was certain both women had also dropped to their knees and scurried to a safer place.

The barrage of bullets was less this time. Moaning from the wounded and damned in the street grew louder.

"Hold your fire!" men shouted in shrill voices.

"I'm hit. Get a doctor." But the gunshots continued and dust rose in the jail from the chipping of the thick adobe.

The air fast became heavy with a fog of bitter dust and gun smoke. The three of them coughed until they cried. Vince soaked his kerchief in the water and handed it to May.

Betty ripped up her skirt and handed him cloths for them to use as masks. Still, the firing continued. Back in the jail cells, his prisoners cursed, but Vince had no cares for them. The mental pressure of the constant shooting was taking a toll on the three of them. Concern etched both women's faces. Their involuntary shuddering and somber masks told him enough.

Then there was silence. Except for the crash when the riddled jail house sign fell down out in front. Vince blinked his burning eyes. From his peep hole he could see men coming out of the wagon with their hands up. He spotted the bald-faced horse and John. Waving a rifle and motioning for some more to surrender were Mark and a dozen white men.

"What's happening?" May coughed as he helped her up.

"It's the boys," he said, shaking his head in disbelief. He shared a private nod with Betty, who was impatient for him to open the steel front door.

"How did they do this?" May asked, hugging his waist.

"There! See that man on the big gray horse?" Vince pointed to the rider coming down the main street herding several prisoners.

"That's Marshal Brooks," Vince said.

"Hello again." The lawman laughed. "I was sitting having me a nice cool beer when this telegraph operator ran in and asked if I was Marshal Brooks. He said they'd sent a telegram to Florence for me and he just knowed I was not ten miles down the line from here at *Aqua Caliente*. So I deputized a few men to bring along. Tell me all about this. Them two Indians of yours sure need some lessons in Spanish or English, but they savvy." Brooks pulled on the ends of his mustache.

"You didn't get here any too soon," Vince said. "I've got Pick Walters's killers locked in the jail. I'm sure they'll implicate Kyle Allison."

"Sounds good enough." Brooks dismounted and stretched his back. "How come every time I see the two of you, I always think I'm seeing someone else?" He shook his head. "I've got to be wrong. You've risked life and limb here, Vince Wagner. I'm proud to know you."

"Did Allison get away?" Vince asked, searching around.

"Nope. We knew for a long time his operation was running heavy-handed. So I figured he was behind the trouble up here and I stopped there first. I've got him leg-ironed in his office where I found him cleaning out his safe. He was fixing to leave in a big hurry. See, you'd probably have won without me."

"Maybe, maybe not." Vince smiled and hugged May under his arm. "I might have, but you made it a damn sight easier."

Vince looked at the dust- and gunpowder-streaked faces of May, Betty, and the two Apaches. "What the Sam Hill you all waiting on? We got cows scattered from here to the Mogollon Rim. The law can handle this.

I want to go home."

Their grins warmed him. He climbed on the buckboard and took the reins. "We'll see you Marshal Brooks." He gave May his hand to pull her up beside him on the spring seat.

"You all right to drive?" she asked with a frown.

"Yes. Let's go home Missus Wagner."

Vince glanced around at the dusty street lined with stores and buildings. New Field held nothing for them. The cool wind of the mountains would be a welcome relief. The three Apaches and his wife had a ranch to carve out. He clucked to the horses and then he hugged May's shoulder. His three Apaches on horseback were even smiling.

Why, they'd be home in no time.

ABOUT THE AUTHOR

Dusty Richards grew up riding horses and watching his western heroes on the big screen. He even wrote book reports for his classmates, making up westerns since English teachers didn't read that kind of book. But his mother didn't want him to be a cowboy, so he went to college, then worked for Tyson Foods and auctioned cattle when he wasn't an anchor on television.

But his lifelong dream was to write the novels he loved. He sat on the stoop of Zane Grey's cabin and promised that he'd get published. And in 1992, his first book, Noble's Way, hit the shelves. Since then, he's had 151 more come out.

If he can steal some time, he also likes to fish for trout on the White River.

Facebook: westernauthordustyrichards
www.dustyrichardslegacy.com